THE MASKED MAN

With his face concealed behind an iron mask, a very important prisoner was kept incarcerated in a number of fortresses throughout France from 1669 to 1703. Ralph Croft, an English rogue, is plucked from the dungeons of the Bastille to head an investigation into the true identity of the masked man. Croft has to face brutal imprisonment, secret assassinations, threats and countless dangers before discovering the truth.

P. C. DOHERTY

THE MASKED MAN

Complete and Unabridged

LINFORD
Leicester

First published in Great Britain in 1991 by
Robert Hale Limited
London

First Linford Edition
published March 1994
by arrangement with
Robert Hale Limited
London

British Library CIP Data

Doherty, P. C.
    The masked man.—Large print ed.—
    Linford mystery library
    I. Title II. Series
    823.914 [F]

    ISBN 0–7089–7482–1

Published by
F. A. Thorpe (Publishing) Ltd.
Anstey, Leicestershire

Set by Words & Graphics Ltd.
Anstey, Leicestershire
Printed and bound in Great Britain by
T. J. Press (Padstow) Ltd., Padstow, Cornwall

This book is printed on acid-free paper

To my secretary,
Grace Harding,
many thanks

Introduction

THE story of the Man in the Iron Mask (besides Alexandre Dumas' great classic) has inspired countless books on the subject. It may come as a surprise to realise that the Man in the Iron Mask is not legend but based on sound historical fact. During the reign of Louis XIV (the Sun King of France) a very important prisoner was kept incarcerated in a number of prison fortresses throughout France from 1669 to 1703. No one except his gaoler was allowed access to him. He was kept under close confinement. His gaolers, who were never changed, had orders to shoot him if he attempted to speak to anyone and, whenever he was transported from one prison to another or took exercise, he wore either a velvet or an iron mask.

The simple facts are as follows. The

1

masked man was arrested near Dieppe in 1669, taken to Pignerol under the custody of Saint Mars who was to be his gaoler for the next thirty years. From Pignerol the masked man was moved to the prisons of Sainte Marguerite, Les Exiles and, finally, the Bastille in Paris. His gaolers for 35 years were the same people and many of them died mysterious deaths. The masked prisoner was buried in St Paul's graveyard near the Bastille but rumour has it that the corpse was decapitated and the coffin strewn with acid before it was interred.

Throughout the Masked Man's imprisonment, his security was entrusted to no less a person than Louis XIV's own Minister of War, who ensured that special cells were built at every prison the Masked Man stayed in. There are many rumours of the true identity of this man. Was he the twin brother of Louis XIV? Was he Louis XIV himself and someone substituted for the King? Was he the Duke of Monmouth, who was executed on Tower Hill in London after an abortive attempt to seize the English throne? Was he the Duke of Lorraine? The idol of the secret order of the Templars.

This novel, *The Masked Man*, examines all these theories through the eyes of an English rogue, the forger, Ralph Croft, who is plucked from the dungeons of the Bastille to head an investigation into the true identity of the masked man. Croft has to work with the mysterious archivist, Monsieur Maurepas, his beautiful, enigmatic daughter, Marie, and the cold killer, Captain D'Estivet. Croft's quest takes him from the poverty of the slums of 18th century Paris to the opulent luxuries of the Louvre Palace. Croft has to face brutal imprisonment, secret assassinations, threats and countless dangers before discovering the truth. *The Masked Man* is a detective novel based on original records and reaches an original solution which can be proved, for Doherty has decoded a royal love letter which may reveal the true identity of the man in the iron mask, and reveals a mystery which, in its time, would have rocked the throne of France.

1

MY name is Scaramouche. No, I change my mind, it's Scaramac, or is it James Stewart the lost King of England? Or Henrietta Maria? Or even Admiral William Penn who sailed off across the Western Seas to find a new world? Nothing is real. We all live behind masks. I will write in English for I am an Englishman. I am Ralph Croft, born in the year 1685 in the parish of St Botolph near Tregoze in Cornwall, the only child of a careless father and a mother who lived long enough to give me birth. I was not an intelligent boy but sharp-witted, a born mimic; someone who could pick up an accent, a trait, a mode of walking as easy as any other child could a sweetmeat. I was eighteen when I ran away to London. Why, you may ask? Well, for three reasons: first, I was bored. Secondly, I was frightened and, thirdly, I just wanted to escape from the full openness, the green flatness of the south-western countryside. No real excitement there except for the fairs, the horse sales and, of course, the sea, angry, boiling with fury, crashing violently against the rocks. I was frightened because the sea led me to the smugglers. Somerset and Cornwall have two trades, agriculture and the import of fine wines, exquisite lace and the best of French brandy, imported, of course, without custom and excise. Boat-loads of these were brought in at the dead of night when the sea whispered far away along the strand and no one watched from the dark, forbidding cliffs.

I was a member of such a gang working at night, waist-high in cold, salty water as we pushed the lugger boats in and unloaded their precious burdens on to waiting carts. Everyone knew because everyone was involved, be it squire, magistrate, parson or landlord. But we became too greedy and London sent down a revenue officer, soldiers and mounted dragoons. At first they kept watch but we slipped through them like eels between the rocks so they posted rewards all around the county and a traitor was found. Good men were imprisoned, even better ones hanged or transported to the colonies in Virginia and New England. I knew who the traitor was, William Bodmin, a lawyer's clerk. One night in 'The Sea Barque', drunk till his face was flushed red and his eyes glittered like cheap marbles, Bodmin leered at me across the taproom, his face devilish in the light of the swinging lantern horns. I took out a pistol I always carried, walked across the taproom, raised the pistol and, cocking back the hammer, pointed it straight at Bodmin's head. I savoured a few seconds of triumph as the Judas' flesh-lipped mouth sagged with disbelief. God knows I only meant to frighten him but I, too, was drunk

7

and my hand was slippery with sweat; the gun was cocked, I let the hammer go and watched as the ball smashed Bodmin's skull into a bloody mess. I fled because I did not want to hang, be strung up in chains at some crossroads, black and tarred for the crows to feast on and little boys in the parish to laugh at. I also wanted to get away from my father who had married again and my stepmother had a hard face with a tongue to match, like a sword every ready to cut. So I was pleased to go. In a week I was in London and, within a month, I was apprenticed to a parchment seller and printer who had one shop under the Red Sign near the Palace of Westminster and another in Chancery Lane close to the courts.

I found I had a gift for writing in a courtly hand, be it in ink or copperplate, as well as for printing. At first, books, bills of sale and notices, but again I became bored and drifted into the thieves' kitchen in Alsatia where there were villains ready to use my skills. Jacobites, men who supported the exiled Stewarts, the kings across the water; these rebels hated fat George from Hanover and constantly plotted to bring him down. They needed their books and pamphlets and, when their cause was defeated, forged papers and licences so they could slip easily back to France. Again greed brought me down and well does Chaucer say how "Avarice is the root of all evil.' I became careless over one customer, a sharp-eyed, thin-lipped cove. He, too, wanted papers and a passport but he turned out to be a government spy, an agent out to trap the unwary. An acquaintance in the Lord Chancellor's office tipped me the wink that warrants would soon be out for my arrest. I took my gold and silver, packed my inks, pens and my few belongings and three days later I was in Le Havre.

I thought of joining some mercenary troop, but who wants to die young? So I followed the Seine up to Paris. The English colony there was large enough for a man to set up shop and do an honest day's business but there is something perverse in me. I quickly picked up the tongue and moved into that pimple on the arse of the world, the Faubourg Saint-Antoine, near the church of St Paul's which lies within spitting distance of the Bastille prison. What horrors I heard about that great, eight-towered medieval fortress, gaunt and sombre; a perpetual shadow against the Parisian sky with its huge towers, muckstained curtain wall and broad, slimy moat. I used to wonder what secrets it held, perhaps even then I had a presentiment of what was to come. Anyway, I started my own printing press, forging notes, bills, anything the customer wanted. I acquired a modicum of wealth and a spacious room above an apothecary's shop.

Of course, I had my brushes with the law and eventually drew the attention of the Chief Provost of Police. I was arrested on a list of counterfeit charges which read as long as a psalm and I was committed to the hell-hole of Montmartre prison. Luckily I had enough wealth to buy a comfortable cell and even more gold to bribe my escape. I should have known better, gone to earth like some fox and hid for a while, but not Ralph Croft. I strode around like some cock on a dunghill, celebrated my escape, arranging parties, buying costly coats and turning up at the opera arm-in-arm with two of the capital's costliest whores. I love music, adore singing, especially the Italian mode, and I was grateful that the police at least waited until the end of the last great chorus, before arresting me as I came out of my own privately hired box. This time I was taken back to Montmartre, where my lovely coat and pantaloons were seized by an irate chief gaoler. I was loaded with chains and a week later, dressed only in my drawers, I heard the gravelly voice of a judge pass sentence of death on me. I was not to be hanged but broken at the wheel at Monfaucon.

Oh, God knows, I would hang but I had not visualised the horrors of being strapped to a huge wheel and slowly turned whilst two thugs smashed my limbs to a bloody pulp. The judge had also heard about my escape from Montmartre and ordered me to be kept in the Bastille until sentence was carried out. Loaded with chains, a squad of soldiers took me from the Palais de Justice back through my old haunts in Saint Antoine, up across the great drawbridge and into the courtyard of the Bastille where skinny chickens pecked amongst piles of refuse. The place smelt as sweet as a dirty whore's breath. However, I kept smiling because I was frightened, especially when the sentries on duty took off their hats and covered their faces the moment they saw me. A strange custom for the soldiers are forbidden to look directly at any prisoner; first, so that faces can never be remembered. Secondly, soldiers are superstitious animals and anyone bound for the Bastille had the mark of death on him.

A turnkey unlocked my chains and pushed me up some steps into the governor's chamber. This was a large, circular room, the floor covered with stained carpets, the walls draped with blue damask, holed and moth-eaten, its gold fringes dirty and worn. The governor stood in front of a roaring fire and inspected me like some cold-eyed crow does a wandering worm. A skinny, short man with the face of a tired horse and manners to boot. At first he received me politely enough, reaching out a trembling hand which felt like a lump of dirty ice. A bad sign, I thought to myself. Death himself is greeting me. The governor took the judge's sentence which the turnkey now carried, read it carefully and his manner changed dramatically enough. I suppose he realised I would not be staying long and there would be little profit to be had from me.

"Take him away!" he squeaked. "The

lowest cell in the Treasure Tower!"
And, before I could protest, I was
bundled out of the room.

My dungeon was simply hell on
earth; cold, wet and black with no
windows or vents for air, whilst the
floor was covered by a greenish-black
mess which seeped in from the moat.
I was thrown there and, after two
days of fighting huge rats which swam
like fish, execution at Monfaucon did
not seem too dreadful. Oh, yes, I
blubbered. I begged for mercy but
no bastard heard me. I prayed to God
but ended up cursing him. I wished for
Cornwall, its green hills sloping down
to the rocky coast, but I remembered
my stepmother's hatchet face and I
thought again. I hummed a ditty from
the opera, dreamt of Danielle, a sweet
girl whom I had pursued like a lecher.
I woke to find a rat squirming on my
leg, staring at me in the dim light,
its huge ears back against its black,
slimy head, and its eyes, two pebbles
of red, gleaming hate. So I screamed,

it scurried away and I began to pray again.

I was supposed to be there a week before I was executed. I made scratches on the wall to mark the days and wondered when eight had passed what had happened. Perhaps a pardon? Perhaps they had just forgotten about me?

I lost control of my soul and my mind, unhinged, drifted like a masterless ship into the great sea of madness. I thought I saw Abigail (she was a girl I had married in London, who took my gold and fled) standing in the far corner of my cell. She was as sweet and treacherous as ever. She smiled and talked to me but I cursed her. One day Abigail came back dressed in strange clothes so I swore at her, lashing out and hitting her on the chest. Then I blinked, laughing wildly, as I realised this was no phantasm but flesh and blood. I struck again and received a stinging slap across my face. I sobered, gathered my wits and looked up at an officer dressed in the uniform of the Swiss mercenaries who man the Bastille. The fellow smiled at me, struck me once, twice across the face and ordered me to follow him. After that, well as Saint Paul says, (remember I did attend Sunday School at St Botolph's) I was changed 'in a twinkling of an eye." I was dragged out of the dungeon, shouting foul obscentities at the phantasms which lurked there, and bundled up into the courtyard.

Christ, it was freezing but delightful; air as fresh as wine just uncorked, the chickens looked as splendid as princes and the dungheaps were only fresh powder for Mother Nature's succulent body. I was stripped naked as a babe and washed down by two grinning, burly musketeers before being pushed into a wash-house where I was dumped into a tub of greasy hot water. Some clothes were thrown at me and a bowl of chicken broth and a cup of watered wine were thrust into my hands. A soldier watched me eat and drink before telling me in guttural French to sleep in the soldier's dormitory. I slept like a baby. My optimism which springs continually in my blackened heart told me something was about to happen. I was free of my stepmother, not going to Monfaucon and, above all, out of that dreadful dungeon.

I was roused long after dark by a soldier, a captain of the royal musketeers by the blue and red facing of his jacket, spotless white breeches and brown polished boots. I rose, sleepy-eyed, stepped into a pool of light and looked into the thin, pale face of Captain D'Estivet, a man I would come to know well. Even then I thought him strange; he had the face of a scholar, hooded eyes and well formed features under his silver wig and large tricorne hat. Ah well, it just goes to show, never judge a bastard by his clothes! In curt tones he ordered me outside where a carriage waited, the lanterns on either side winking through the darkness. I climbed in and D'Estivet joined me.

He ensured the windows were covered by their leather flaps, tapped on the ceiling with his fingers and the carriage rumbled across the drawbridge on to the cobbled street beyond. I heard the sound of water, the shouts of bargemen and realised we were following the river Seine. During the journey D'Estivet did not even bother to look at me, let alone speak, but sat swathed in his cloak, lost in his own thoughts. Again I heard the sound of sentries grounding their muskets, gates being opened and the glimpse of an occasional torch. D'Estivet, lounging in the corner, stirred himself, pulling back the leather flap, sighed and tapped once more on the ceiling. The carriage stopped, D'Estivet opened the door, indicating we should get out. I looked around, the cobbled courtyard was bathed in the light of torches fixed in huge iron sockets. I gasped at the cold night air, looked up and recognised the turrets and rounded towers of the Louvre Palace and, in the distance, above the crenellated walls, the huge twin towers of Notre Dame Cathedral.

An officer, resplendent in a golden jerkin and scarlet hose, approached, listened attentively to D'Estivet's murmured request and led us up a flight of broad steps into a huge hall where candlelight shimmered on marble floors. I remember a mural on the ceiling depicting the Goddess of Love and I would have liked to admire her rich breasts but D'Estivet pushed me forward, following the officer up a curving marble staircase and through a bewildering maze of chambers. In one, a billiard board as broad as a small paddock; in another, tables arranged in horseshoe fashion, groaned under a buffet, plate after plate of cold meats and high, silver vases used for hot and cold drinks, fruit juice, wine, chocolate and coffee. My starved stomach protested in anger, rumbling so loudly that even D'Estivet must have heard it.

Finally, we entered the Salon de

Mars. The entire ceiling was carved with the God of War in a chariot drawn by ravenous wolves. At the far end of the room there was a huge marble fireplace, its massive gabled hood reached high up the wall, almost touching the red, gold and blue gobelin tapestries hanging there. These seemed to dwarf the two figures sitting in tall-backed chairs before the fire. The officer led us forward, his feet clicking on the marble floor. One of the figures stirred and got up, his face red, full and fleshy under a silver white periwig. He just stood there in a long robe fashioned out of costly purple silk, fringed with gold-dyed lambswool. The woman sitting beside him had turned at our approach. She had the same puffy face as her companion, with shrewd, dark eyes and a stern Roman nose.

"On your knees before the Regent!" D'Estivet murmured as he bowed on one leg. I needed no second bidding but crouched in astonishment. The officer who had led us up clicked his heels and quickly withdrew. I just knelt there. The woman giggled and stopped as the Regent tutted, whispering something so fast I could not catch it.

"Your Graces," D'Estivet said, drawing himself to his full height. "May I present Scaramac, better known to the authorities as the English forger, Ralph Croft!"

"Tell him to get up! Tell him to get up!" The voice was peevish. The Regent turned away, picked up a small bell and he had hardly finished tinkling it when a far door opened and servants brought in two chairs which they gently placed between the Regent and his companion. I felt abashed at such company and rather frightened. What did the Duke of Orleans, Regent of France, nephew of the glorious King Louis XIV and guardian of the latter's heir-apparent, the boy Louis, want with me? I glanced up and caught the Regent's lazy eyes studying me, noticing how his cheeks were rouged, his lips carmine painted and twisted in a grimace of distaste.

I looked sideways; the woman, too, was watching me. She was old but imperious and her ravaged face still bore traces of her earlier beauty.

"Captain D'Estivet," the Regent remarked. "Your guest." The word was laced with sarcasm. "Your guest knows who we are?"

"He knows he is in the presence of greatness, your Grace. He has undoubtedly recognised Monsieur Le Duc but, Madame de Maintenon, now he knows her name, will also mean something to him."

Oh, I knew them well enough. Madame had been the mistress of King Louis XIV, as much a feature of court life as the Louvre Palace she was sitting in. The Duke of Orleans was also no stranger to the gossips and scandalmongers of the St Antoine. Was he not, so rumour had it, in love with his own daughter, the Duchess of Berry? And, only a few years before the old King's death had he not been accused of poisoning the Duke and Duchess of Bourgogne?

The ravaged, dissipated face of this ancient roué studied me carefully.

"So, you know who we are, Croft?" he remarked. "And we also know who you are." He turned to a small, ivory, inlaid table which stood beside his chair and gingerly picked up a yellowing piece of parchment. He unfolded it as if unwilling to soil his hands, glanced at me and read it out aloud. "Wanted," he intoned, "in London and the county of Cornwall for murder, counterfeiting and smuggling. Ralph Croft, aged about twenty eight, five foot eleven inches in height, with dark reddish hair, white face, green eyes, of medium build, a consummate liar and publicly proclaimed villain. The Sheriffs of London and Cornwall are willing to pay one hundred pounds sterling for his capture."

Orleans tossed the piece of paper into the fire, watching the flames turn it into a black, feathery cinder.

"In England, Monsieur, you are wanted, and in France you are caught! You should have died three days ago at Monfaucon but this," he turned once more to the table and picked up a small scroll tied with green silk. "This is a pardon for duties you will perform for us." He smiled, displaying teeth, jagged, yellow and ill set. "You may try to escape but, if you do, D'Estivet will kill you. If he fails, others will capture you. If you go to England, you will hang. If you flee elsewhere, my agents will track you down and either kill you or bring you back!" Orleans touched the beauty spot high on his right, sunken cheek. "You are an accomplished rogue, Croft, I prefer that name to Scaramac, the alias you took in Paris. I have seen your forgeries. Fine examples of criminal art. You are good with paper, with printing, with secret dyes and inks. We can use you."

He picked up the bell, again the silver tinkling and the door opened. I glanced around and saw a servant bring in a third chair, which he placed at the other side of D'Estivet. Behind the servant stood a tall man, dressed in a dark brown suit. I caught a glimpse of black, shiny shoes, a tricorne hat and a cuff of exquisitely ruffled silk. Orleans did not bother to introduce this newcomer but nodded and told him to sit.

"You are all here," the Regent began, "the three of you, D'Estivet, Captain of my personal guard, Monsieur Maurepas, master of my library and archives, and this," he flicked a lace-edged hand towards me, "this English forger." He seemed to like the phrase, grinned, and I noticed how his eye teeth were stained black. "You are here to take an oath."

Madame de Maintenon held out a huge book bound in black, red and gold leather. The Regent nodded.

"You will swear!"

First, Maurepas, then D'Estivet and finally myself. I swore to God knows what. As I took my hand away I glanced sideways at the archivist. A scholar, I thought, noting the full lugubrious face, thin lips and dark, short-sighted eyes which crinkled with amusement as he caught my gaze.

Orleans sighed.

"The task," he began, "the one you have sworn to, is known to two of you. Monsieur Maurepas and Captain D'Estivet." He licked his lips. "You are sworn to discover the true identity of the Man in the Iron Mask."

I froze. Even I, a foreigner, an outlaw, had heard the rumours about a secret, mysterious prisoner who had spent the greater part of Louis XIV's reign in a number of fortress prisons, his face always hidden behind an iron mask.

"You may ask why," the Regent continued quietly, "but that is not your concern. How? Well, you will be given access and allowed to study all the letters of my deceased uncle, the King; all state secret letters, memoranda, ciphers." He waved his hand airily.

"Etc. etc. Maurepas, you have been chosen for your skill as an archivist and because I trust you. D'Estivet, you are a soldier, a skilled guardsman, your task will be to protect your companions. And you, Englishman, you are here not only because of your criminal skills, but because of your acquaintance with the secret ways of the city. You are a criminal but you can work for your pardon. You, Croft, will stay here. You will want for nothing and your custody is entrusted to Captain D'Estivet."

He looked at us all in one sweeping glance.

"Be wary!" he added.

"Yes, be wary," repeated the old woman, turning her wrinkled face towards us. "Be most wary and do not talk!"

She rose, flouncing out her old-fashioned skirts around her and walked away without a backward glance. The Regent collected a few documents lying on the table, he handed my pardon to Maurepas and followed Madame de Maintenon out of the room. The door closed behind them and we just sat staring into the flames. I could hardly believe my good fortune. I had escaped death and prison. Oh, I looked at D'Estivet's close face and had no illusions about him. He would kill me and probably enjoy doing it; nor had I any fanciful ideas about my final fate. It would be easy for an Englishman, let alone one convicted for forgery in a French court, to quietly disappear. Many strange things are fished out of the Seine. I did not wish to be one of these but I decided to live for the day and confront that danger when it arose.

"Come!" Maurepas rose, he smiled and I noticed his eyes, though myopic, were kind and full of good humour. He led me and D'Estivet down to the kitchen. The huge, lime-washed rooms were quiet, the massive ovens, stoves and kitchen ranges cold. Maurepas, however, using his authority and showing a warrant which the Regent must have given him, roused the cook and two scullion boys from their truckle beds in the far corner. After much grumbling and protests we were served soup, bread and cold chicken with some white wine drawn from a barrel. Maurepas and D'Estivet picked at their meals, all the time watching me wolf down my food. Afterwards Maurepas led us back upstairs, further up into the palace; guards resplendent in blue, red and white facings, stopped us but stepped hastily back when Maurepas showed his warrant.

"Signed by the Regent himself!" Maurepas smugly commented. "It gives me access to any room or building except for the royal apartments. D'Estivet has one too. You," he smiled, "will never have one. You understand?"

He did not wait for an answer but showed me into a small chamber at the top of the palace, furnished with a bed, its hangings costly but sloppy. Beside it was a leather-backed chair and beneath the window, a broad oak desk with a stool. On the floor was a Persian carpet though the fringes were ragged and dirty and the colour in the centre quite faded. I noticed a mousetrap, the bloody remains of some rodent still caught there. Perhaps it was the dirt, the quietness of D'Estivet, the smugness of Maurepas but I picked up the mousetrap and, as an act of defiance, opened the shutter and tossed it through a small window, not caring where it fell. I then went to shake both their hands and grinned as they stepped back. Maurepas nodded.

"We shall see you in the morning. Shall we say nine o'clock?"

As soon as they were gone I climbed on to the bed and slept fitfully. I woke in the early hours to relieve myself in the chamber pot. I silently opened my door and looked out. Surprisingly, the Regent did not trust me. Two guards stood there, bayonets fixed. I closed the door and went back to bed, fully committed to the task which had rescued me from the dark dungeons of the Bastille.

2

THE guards were still there in the morning and one, a friendly but close shadow, followed me down to the kitchen, where I begged some food; bread dipped in honey, a huge bowl of sweetened black coffee and a cup of red wine to settle my stomach. The kitchen was now busy with sweating cooks, scullions and maids hurrying about in a mixture of steam, smoke and the mingling odours of freshly baked bread, roast chicken, herbs and other meat. I looked up at a huge clock fashioned in the Swiss manner, the glass face was misted over but the guard lounging behind me shouted,

"It is nine o'clock, Monsieur!"

I wandered up into the same entrance vestibule I had entered the previous evening. Now it was thronged with resplendent courtiers, even at that early hour, hurrying to attend some engagement or hoping for an invitation to the Regent's levée. I watched a group standing round a small table drinking chocolate, laughing and talking without a care in the world. Butterflies, I thought, brilliant and beautiful, flitting from one occasion to another; a theatre, an opera, a soirée, a masque. Nothing substantial. I thought of the poverty of the Faubourg Saint-Antoine and wondered how long the two worlds could exist cheek by jowl. I looked around. The guard had gone, instead D'Estivet was there, dressed in a plain, grey suit with matching hose, the only concession to fashion being his lace-edged shirt and high-heeled, buckled shoes. He bade good morning and took me up rows of stairs through halls and chambers to a spacious library. The floor was of polished wood and the walls were covered with shelf after shelf of books all bound in different types of leather. Maurepas joined us and invited us to sit round the huge table on which he placed a small coffer, iron-bound and secured with two padlocks.

"The Regent," he began, "has given us two months to find all there is to know about the identity of the Man in the Iron Mask." He tapped the small coffer and cleared his throat. "We know several facts. First the man died in the Bastille on November 19th 1703. Secondly, we know the prisoner was incarcerated in gaols throughout France for the previous thirty years. He was in the custody of one gaoler. Etienne Saint-Mars, who moved him from Pignerol to Les Exiles from there to Sainte Marguerite and, finally, in 1698, to the Bastille."

"How do we know that?" I interrupted.

Maurepas tapped the small coffer again.

"I have done some initial work."

"Where was the corpse buried?" I asked.

"In the churchyard of St Paul's," Maurepas answered, "just outside the

Bastille." He smiled at me. "The very church you would have visited, Monsieur Croft, before you would have been taken out to Monfaucon." He shrugged. "Ça ira — that's all in the past." Maurepas took a small ring of keys from his belt and unlocked the coffer, drawing out a piece of parchment which he handed to me. "Captain D'Estivet has already seen this: it is a copy of the death certificate drawn up and signed after the masked prisoner died in the Bastille. It is signed by Major Rosarges, an officer of the Bastille; and Monsieur Reilhe, who served as both doctor and surgeon there."

I read the certificate carefully.

"*On November 19th, Marciel, aged 45 or thereabouts, died at the Bastille. His body was buried in the cemetery of St Paul's, his parish, on the 20th of the present month, in the presence of M. Rosarges, the Major of the Bastille, and of M. Reilhe, surgeon of the Bastille, who signed; Rosarges, Reilhe.*"

"But you said the man was in prison for at least thirty years and that his name was not known!" I exclaimed. "Yet here he has a name, Marciel, and his age is given as forty-five! You are not going to ask me to believe that Louis XIV imprisoned a boy of fifteen!"

Maurepas agreed.

"This is why you are here, Monsieur Croft. The record is valid but the facts have been twisted. I doubt if he was forty-five years of age or that his name was Marciel or, as some say, Marchiele. There is no record of such a man. The only fact this certificate tells us is that he died, the rest is a lie."

I looked out through the window: the spring morning was darkening and a strengthening wind lashed the rain drops against the glass. I shivered and wondered what doors were opening for me now. I mean, I am a professional liar, a forger who has to counterfeit; but why should a great king take such pains to ensure a poor man's death certificate did not tell the truth?

"Moreover," Maurepas continued catching my attention, "we know this document is lying because here," he drew out a second document, "is the official extract from the register at the Bastille. No name is given. The extract reads as follows. Go on, read it!"

He passed the extract, on which a sprawled hand had copied from the register: *"Ancient prisoner of Pignerol, always obliged to wear a mask of black velvet, of whom nothing has ever been known about his name or qualities."*

I threw the document back as Maurepas leaned on the table, steepling his fingers, now looking at D'Estivet lounging in his chair. The soldier looked bored but I knew this was just an affected air.

"I have already said this to D'Estivet," Maurepas remarked, turning to me. "But I will repeat it for your benefit. One explanation we must demolish is that the prisoner was a twin brother of King Louis XIV, our glorious monarch now deceased, whose heir is soon to come of age." He glanced around the room as if he half-suspected the walls did have ears and lowered his voice. "Such an explanation is the most popular story and to understand it we must go back over a hundred years. In 1615 Louis XIII, the great-grandfather of the present Regent, married Anne of Austria, but our real story does not begin until 1638 when Anne became pregnant. Two shepherds came to Paris. They sought an audience with the King and warned him that they both had seen a vision in which they had been told how Queen Anne would give birth to twin boys who would divide and annihilate France in a vicious civil war over who should wear the crown. The King, a superstitious man, took the prophecy to heart." Maurepas stopped speaking and waved his hand at me. "Please do not interrupt me, I know you are going to ask why should a King talk to shepherds? You must remember that in the history of the French crown the role of the shepherd prophet has played a decisive role. Anyway, the King went to seek advice from his Chief Minister, Cardinal Richelieu; the Cardinal, although a man of God, took the shepherds' warning lightly and had both men locked up in the asylum of St Lazaire. On the 9th of September 1638, the Queen was brought to bed and gave birth to a son, the future Louis XIV, in the presence of all the witnesses which law and etiquette demanded. King Louis XIII was overjoyed but at four in the afternoon, whilst resting on his couch, the midwife, Dame Perronet, informed him that the Queen's labour pains had recommenced. Now seriously alarmed, Louis, accompanied by Richelieu, hastened back to the bedside to witness his Queen give birth to a second son, much more handsome and vigorous than the first. King Louis, bearing in mind the prophecy of the shepherds, ordered the second child to be handed over to the midwife, who would pretend it was the offspring of some lady-in-waiting."

Maurepas stopped, got up and went across to a table where he half-filled three goblets with wine, before adding a generous supply of water to each. He served both D'Estivet and myself before downing one cup and continuing.

"The second child was raised in secrecy by one of Louis' favourites in the town of Dijon. The boy's suspicions, so the story goes, were first alerted by the incredible deference the nobleman showed him and by the fact that he was never allowed to see a portrait of the King. At the same time, his guardian kept up a secret correspondence with Anne of Austria. The young man intercepted one of these letters and, using his charm and guile, managed to obtain a full portrait of Louis XIV. The young man now realised his true identity and sought an interview with his mother and twin brother. Louis XIV, however, alarmed and frightened at a potential rival to his crown, ordered his twin brother to be seized, wear an iron mask and be incarcerated for his natural life in one prison after another." Maurepas stopped.

I was too busy reflecting on what he had said but Captain D'Estivet leaned forward.

"I agree that this story is the popular one. But why should we disbelieve it?"

"First," Maurepas replied, "Anne of Austria's accouchement and birth were watched and witnessed by literally dozens of people at court. Anything untoward would have been reported. Secondly, Richelieu was not present at the time, he was away on the King's business. Thirdly, why should Louis XIII discard a twin son? How many baby boys live past the age of five? He had no guarantee that the first boy might not die in infancy. It would be feckless to reject a legitimate, healthy, male heir. Fourthly, Louis XIII had brothers; Louis XIV had brothers and, undoubtedly, the future Louis XV's heir will have brothers, they pose no real threat. Finally, the story is preposterous and ignores any parental feelings on the part of Louis and Anne towards a healthy male boy."

"Yes," I said, "but why was the prisoner masked? You say it was an iron mask? Yet I noticed the register from the Bastille says the mask was velvet."

Maurepas shrugged.

"Perhaps a steel one was worn at certain times when there was danger of someone seeing him and the velvet one when the prisoner was locked away."

Maurepas chewed his lower lip, rose and walked to where a leather sack was thrown in the far corner. He picked it up, brought it back and gently emptied the contents out on to the table. First, a key about three inches long and, finally, an iron mask: Maurepas turned the dented, marked face towards me. It measured about eight to nine inches from top to bottom, about seven inches across and was fashioned out of hammered plate with cut-out eyes, nostrils and mouth. The upper rim was thinned, there were three holes in the forehead and the lower edge was perforated with holes along the entire length. There were gaps in the ear section. The back was shaped roughly in the form of a skull and the whole contrivance was locked in the side just above the neck.

"Is this the mask?" I asked.

"We don't know," Maurepas replied. "The Regent gave it to me. He said it came from the Bastille." Maurepas stood up and examined my head. "You wear no wig, Monsieur Croft, and your hair is newly cropped from your stay in the Montmartre. Perhaps you will do us the courtesy?"

And, before I could object, he opened the mask up and, watched by a grinning D'Estivet, lowered it over my face. The two sides were brought together and I caught my breath as Maurepas inserted the key and turned it. I had a strange feeling of being in the world but not there, almost like a ghost. I could see, hear and smell everything around me but my face, my features, my thoughts, my expressions were hidden from my two companions. The mask felt light and was made out of very fine steel, probably from some foundry in Milan or Turin. It caught me a little on the right ear. I felt a slight tightness under my chin but no physical discomfort, just a deep disquiet.

"Take it off!" I rasped, glaring at Maurepas. "Take it off!"

The archivist smiled, the key was inserted and I gasped with relief as the mask was detached and lifted from my head.

"What do you think, Monsieur Croft?"

"I have already asked," I snapped, "why the mask? I can understand a prisoner being locked away in some mountain fortress but why hide his face?" I turned to D'Estivet. "Captain, give me a coin, any one will do!"

D'Estivet smiled and brought out three coins. I took the largest, a silver piece dating from the reign of Louis XIV.

"Look." I said, "the King's face." I turned the coin over and stared at the full profile of Louis XIV, the high cheeks, the arrogant eyes, the curving nose and the luxuriant curling periwig. I handed the coin over to Maurepas. "Everyone knows this face." I said. "Or everyone did. Could it be that the story you relate is the truth, that the masked prisoner bore such a close resemblance to the King that he had to be hidden away? Your story," I concluded, "might well be correct in certain details."

"Such as what?" D'Estivet lazily asked.

"Perhaps the prisoner was an illegitimate son of Louis XIII. Yes, an illegitimate half-brother of Louis XIV."

D'Estivet snorted with laughter.

"For the love of God, Croft!" he replied. "The Kings of France have been known for their bastards! Why,

King Henry IV had more illegitimate children than I have had glasses of wine! Why should one be locked away?"

"Perhaps it was not an illegitimate child of Louis XIII," I replied heatedly, "but of his Queen, Anne of Austria!"

Maurepas tapped me on the wrist.

"I am pleased with you, Ralph." he remarked. "You think quickly but you must also think deeply. Louis XIII did not like his wife. He was deeply suspicious of her; the people did not like her, even when she sold her earrings and bought bread for the poor. A queen is watched, every word, every action. Do you think that she would be allowed to become pregnant, have a child and no one at court notice it?" He shook his head. "I doubt it. Louis XIII was not happy with women, not even his own wife. He was cold, suspicious, a hypochondriac, and he had a tendency to become depressed. Anne was hot-blooded, Spanish in the full sense of the word and Louis XIII had a hatred for Spain which bordered on madness. As I have said, Louis did not like women. When he and Anne were married in 1615 they were both only fourteen years of age and Louis, not Anne, was the one who cried and protested." Maurepas looked around. "They say," he whispered, "that Louis XIII was sexually repressed and did not mature as a man until past his thirtieth year. They say he had no beard and had no necessity to shave until he was past his twenty-fifth year. Do you think such a man, Monsieur Croft, with his dislike of women and hatred of the Spanish, would allow his wife to make him a cuckold?"

I pushed my wine cup towards him as if moving a chess piece.

"My question still stands." I said. "Why was he masked?"

"Perhaps as a punishment," D'Estivet interrupted. "The records show that other prisoners at the Bastille were forced to wear masks. It was a common punishment in Spain and Italy."

"Then let us try another tack," I

said. "The masked prisoner is dead. Louis XIV is dead. Surely the great ones who remain must know the truth?"

Maurepas shook his head.

"No, they do not. The Regent does not. Louis XIV's mistress, Madame de Maintenon, does not." He pulled another sheet of parchment over. This is a copy of a letter written in 1711 by the wife of Louis XIV's brother, the Princess Palatine. She is relating bits of family news and the gossip of the court. This is what she writes — '*A man spent several years in the Bastille and died there wearing a mask. This treatment was probably unavoidable because he was otherwise very well treated, well looked after and given everything he desired. He received the sacrament of communion wearing the mask. He was very devout and read continuously. No one could ever learn who he was.*'"

Maurepas spread his hands. "This is what the great ones of the land know, as much as you or I, Monsieur Croft. So, what do you recommend?"

"When you have forged a document," I began, not caring about D'Estivet stiffening beside me, "you always begin with what is certain, what you are sure of. If you can counterfeit a particular word, begin with that. The same applies here. We have only one certainty."

"Which is?" Maurepas snapped.

"The graveyard at St Paul's," I replied.

Maurepas' face paled.

"Look," I urged, "we must exhume the body. God knows, it is only seventeen years and the coffin might bear some trace or afford some clue. There have been cases of corpses which have not truly decayed. We must begin there. Surely the Regent will give us permission?"

Maurepas was about to disagree but D'Estivet, surprisingly, supported me.

"The Englishman is right," he commented. "The tomb, the grave, the corpse are all we have. Surely his Grace the Regent will give us permission?"

Maurepas leaned back in his chair. "You are right," he said at last. "D'Estivet, you come with me. Monsieur Croft, you will have to stay here until we return!"

They were gone hours and the sky outside the window was beginning to darken before they returned. I whiled the afternoon away walking round the room, reading one or two of the manuscripts. I even opened the door and went into the gallery. I smiled when I saw a serjeant of the Swiss guard at the far end of the passageway, leaning against a pillar watching me as if he were a cat and I the long awaited mouse. A servant brought me something to eat and drink. Between five and six in the evening Maurepas and D'Estivet came back. Both looked excited, their faces flushed, eyes gleaming. Maurepas waved a small piece of parchment he held between his two fingers and I quietly cursed. My wits were dull. Maurepas had left his casket unlocked on the table and never once had I bothered to discover what other secrets it might have held. Perhaps not much. Maurepas went straight into the room, looked at the casket and shrugged before grasping me tightly by the arm.

"We have permission, Croft! The Regent has given us permission and, to quote your Shakespeare — 'if it were done, when 'tis done then 'twere well it were done quickly.' We will exhume the body tonight, after dark!"

We whiled away another two or three hours before Maurepas and D'Estivet led me downstairs, through cavernous galleries and passageways to the rear of the palace. Maurepas mentioned something about men waiting at a postern gate and we found five soldiers, well armed, carrying picks, shovels and flaming torches, waiting for us. The leader of the group saluted D'Estivet.

"We are ready. We have been waiting, Monsieur le Capitain. We are to go where?"

"The graveyard of St Paul's!"

D'Estivet testily remarked, looking up into the night sky. "There is a full moon. The torches will not be necessary until we get there." He glanced sideways at me, his face looking pale, rather drawn. "I have discovered where the grave lies. So, come, let's be done with it!"

We walked down alleyways, narrow streets, all swathed in darkness despite the lantern horns hanging on the corners of houses or above their front doors. Most lawabiding citizens were abed but not so my former friends, those who sleep by day and hunt like rats by night amongst the slums, fetid alleys and shit-strewn runnels of Paris. Now and again I saw shadows flit across our path, movements in the darkness which fell quiet as we approached. In the main we were alone, the boots of the soldiers ringing hollow on the rough-hewn cobbles. Only the occasional scavenging cat and the threatening rustle of rats gnawing in the refuse heaps which littered every street made me jump or start. We came to a crossroads where a huge brazier, built high with flaming charcoal, afforded some light and heat against the cold of the night. I saw a statue of a saint high in its niche and beneath it a six-branched gibbet, like some ghastly tree, its rotten, swaying human fruit macabre shadows against the moonlit sky. The huge mass of St Paul's rose above us. We entered the church's enclosure by a wicket gate and walked down the side of the building into the silent, cypress-filled cemetery beyond. Here we stopped, the soldiers trying to hide their fear under good-humoured banter. Both D'Estivet and Maurepas were apprehensive but I was not concerned, the dead do not bother me. I have enough trouble pitting my wits against the living.

"You can take us to the grave?" I asked.

D'Estivet nodded and led us deeper into the graveyard, pushing his way through the bushes and wet, soft grass. The silence was oppressive as we made our way past mounds of earth; some with headstones, others with battered wooden crosses, a few, just forlorn heaps of clay. As in life, the rich can afford anything, stone memorials exquisitely carved, but the burial places of the poor were not even properly dug; nothing but shallow holes which scarcely concealed their dead, left open to scavenging dogs and other creatures of the night. Time and again we came across heaps of white shard-like bones or tripped, swearing, over a trailing white skeletal limb protruding through its thin veil of soil. An owl hoot made us jump. One of the soldiers cursed as the ghostly bird flew low over our heads, plunging into the grass to grasp some little creature which squealed and squirmed in its death agonies.

"Come on!" D'Estivet ordered urgently. We walked a little further into a far corner of the graveyard to stand beneath a huge cypress tree, its branches splayed out like the ribs of some dark, satanic fan. Only one grave, a wooden cross, thick and heavy but now decayed after years of exposure to rain and wind. No name, no title. Even the mound of earth had almost disappeared.

"This is the grave!" D'Estivet remarked and, taking one of the cresset torches, ordered the soldiers to start digging. Soon all five were hacking and hewing at the rain-soaked earth, piling up heaps of heavy clay on either side of the deepening hole. Most graves are two, three feet deep but the soldiers must have dug at least two yards before we heard the dull thud of one of their spades hitting wood.

"Be careful!" D'Estivet urged.

The soldiers cleared a small space around the coffin. Ropes were lowered. The soldiers scrambled out and, after a great deal of huffing and pulling, the coffin began to rise out from the grave. It bore no insignia, plate or cross though I could see the wood was expensive, heavy and polished before it had been attacked by the passage of time and the ravages of the grave. The soldiers gently rested it on one side of the grave and D'Estivet, using a bayonet, began to prise the lid loose. It creaked and groaned but would not shift. Cursing, D'Estivet tugged at the bottom of the coffin and staggered as the wood broke in his hands. I caught a strange smell, not putrefaction but something sharp and acrid. I knelt down, Maurepas behind me. I looked into that part of the coffin now open and saw a pair of skeletal legs, the bones yellow, the toes and top part of the feet already mouldering into a fine dust. Maurepas shook his head.

"Too soon!" he whispered. "Look!"

D'Estivet joined us and put the torch almost into the coffin. The wood on the bottom and sides looked as it it had been eaten away, stained with some substance. D'Estivet now pulled the rest of the coffin lid off, revealing the skeleton's pelvis and rib cage. All bore the same marks of advancing decomposition and the wood on both sides was a dirty whitish hue. Finally, D'Estivet worked the top part of the lid loose and Maurepas and I both gasped in astonishment. Where we had expected to see a skull, a grinning, sagging jaw, there was nothing but a round black rock; the corpse had been decapitated before burial. The soldiers were now muttering. D'Estivet ordered them to place the wooden slats back over the coffin and it was hurriedly reburied whilst we conferred a short distance away.

"What have we learnt?" I asked.

Maurepas smiled, wiping the sweat from his brow with the cuff of his sleeve.

"I don't know," he muttered. "But two things I am certain of; the corpse had been decapitated and, secondly, we were supposed to find nothing there. The advanced state of decay, the marks on the wood show that before the coffin was lowered into the grave, someone doused the entire contents with more than a generous dose of acid!"

57

3

AFTER dismissing the soldiers, Maurepas and D'Estivet escorted me back to the Louvre Palace. Our journey was quiet, each lost in his own thoughts about the macabre sight we had just witnessed. Maurepas waited outside the palace whilst D'Estivet led me back to my room. I tried to question him on what he thought of the matter but his eyes were troubled, his face white as if he had seen a ghost. He was a source of little advice and even less comfort. My sleep that night was racked by terrible dreams. I was outside the Bastille. The huge fortress was lit by torches but, as I walked across the drawbridge, I felt I was entering a living tomb. The sentries stood, heads bowed in silence. When I approached one, he suddenly snapped back, lifting his face and I stepped away in horror at the grinning skull under the black tricorne hat. I continued into the courtyard where the huge flambeaux flickered hungrily so the figures standing there seemed to leap and turn as if in some macabre dance. I was pushed on, through a heavy iron door at the base of a tower, the steps down were wet with mildew and the smell was putrid with the rottenness of the grave.

I descended through a hellish darkness lit here and there by mysterious fires, down rat-filled passageways and sombre, hollow galleries until I came to a door of thickest oak bound by iron strips and strengthened with huge, steel bosses. On my approach it creaked open on its rusty hinges and I stepped into a vaulted dungeon. The walls were dank and dirty, the air thick, musty and sour. A roaring fire in the middle of the room sent out gusts of heat and light which lit up the far wall where a skeleton hung in chains, its white arms splayed out in a gruesome caricature of the Crucifixtion. The head was bowed. I walked across and saw the iron mask, similar to the one Maurepas had shown me, clamped across its face. I prised it open, my breath held as I waited to glimpse the skull. Instead I screamed in terror at the glowing iron face which glared back at me. I woke, soaked in sweat, and slept only fitfully after that. D'Estivet and Maurepas roused me late in the morning; the captain looked as if he, too, had slept badly, though Maurepas was as cool and calm as ever.

We broke our fast together and walked in the palace gardens. The events of the previous evening had disturbed us all but D'Estivet in particular, who appeared to have lost his frosty haughtiness and regaled us with stories about his military past, so we chattered and laughed like long lost friends meeting to exchange stories and anecdotes. D'Estivet was a Gascon, the son of a wine merchant who had left Bordeaux for Rouen and Paris to serve as a soldier, first in Spain and then in the Low Countries. He was a fount of stories, extolling the virtues of the military life, claiming he had not worsened his state by matrimony — well, not yet. When he said this D'Estivet glanced sideways at Maurepas, who smiled benignly back as if they shared some secret.

It was one of the pleasantest mornings I had spent for years, chatting and gossiping as if such common talk would ease away the terrors of the previous evening. At mid-day bells rang and a cannon sounded; the park became busy, ladies and gentlemen of the court promenading before their afternoon meal. A small Nubian pageboy rushed by, his white turban gleaming in the sun as he chased a ball, splashing mud on his crimson hose and polished leather shoes. The pageboy's antics drew shrieks of laughter and annoyance from a group of ladies gathered like a bunch of beautiful flowers round lace-covered tables where servants were preparing a collation of cooked meats, comfits and huge tumblers of iced white wine. Two carriages thundered by us, each drawn by four black ponies and full of young courtiers who pelted us with apple cores before disappearing in a cloud of dust through a gate leading to a small forest. Their dogs charged after them howling and barking as if part of some hunt. D'Estivet, his face serious, let his hand fall to his sword but Maurepas touched him lightly on the shoulder and we returned to our chamber.

"Last night," Maurepas began, when we were comfortably ensconced in our chairs, "revealed the true nature of the problem. The man we hunt has been carefully concealed and hidden, even in death." He waved his hands at the shelves around us. "We have letters and documents to go through but I am fascinated by Monsieur Croft's logic." He smiled at me. "You told us to go back to the last certainty, the masked prisoner's burial place at St Paul's. Last night we did and learnt nothing. So let us move one pace further forward. We learnt nothing at the grave but perhaps we may discover something at the last prison the masked man stayed in, the Bastille."

D'Estivet immediately agreed. I was more reluctant to visit my old prison. I would have voiced my protest but it would have been ridiculous, a bit like a little boy refusing to go back to the parish school where he was beaten. I had no choice. I took my cloak (Maurepas had been kind enough to provide me with a little money as well as extra clothing) for, though the spring sun was strong, by the time we left the palace, dark clouds were scudding in over the Seine. It felt good to be back amongst the crowds; the shabby shopkeepers who ply their trade from under their striped stalls or from small shop windows let down by chains in front of the houses; these only make the street even narrower. The noise made me dizzy: the crash of cartwheels, the high-pitched calls of the Parisian shopkeepers and the constant chatter, for the French love to discuss everything and have turned conversation into an art. A beggar crawled out from a narrow doorway, hands extended, his lips pouting about the sores and injuries he had received in the late King's wars. He took one look at me, however, and shot back nimbly enough, grinning from ear to ear, and I recognised a brother charlatan, a professional beggar, who claims injuries to both legs due to service in the King's wars. The truth is that his legs are as good as mine and, on occasion, he can (and often has to) move swifter than a greyhound.

We walked under the shifting sky, past the Chatelet and Conciergerie down to the Bastille, its towers soaring up; a brooding presence at the cross-roads, where the broad avenues running along the Seine split into the narrow alleys and streets of the Faubourg St Antoine. We crossed the drawbridge into the fortress. I shivered as I remembered my dream and half expected to find the phantasms waiting for me in the inner courtyard though little seemed to have changed since my last unhappy visit. I drew deep breaths and calmed my nerves. Maurepas demanded to see the captain of the guard, who came bustling out of the barracks, snapping to attention as he recognised D'Estivet. Maurepas murmured a few words, showed him the omnipotent warrant and the fellow ran off. A young officer, probably relaxing after his mid-day meal, came out, buttoning up his jacket, his red face almost puce-like under the regulation snow-white, polished wig.

"Monsieur De Launay?" Maurepas asked.

The man nodded, his watery, blue eyes anxiously watching us. Maurepas handed him the now rather grubby warrant and the soldier's face paled.

"We have questions," D'Estivet commented sharply. "You are a lieutenant?"

De Launay nodded.

"Ye..es." His stammer was quite pronounced. He chewed his lips and looked round nervously.

"We have questions, Lieutenant," D'Estivet continued, "about the famous masked prisoner."

"I was not here then," De Launay murmured.

"No, no, you weren't," D'Estivet interrupted drily. "In fact, there are very few left of those who were, still alive. Is that not so, soldier?" D'Estivet walked closer, ticking the names off on his fingers. "Our masked prisoner died in 1703, his gaoler, Saint-Mars in 1708; Saint-Mars' lieutenant, du Jonca, in 1706; and Saint-Mars' personal lieutenant, Major Rosarges, in 1703 and Surgeon Reilhe in 1710. But you," He tapped the man gently on the chest with his silver-topped walking cane. "You, sir, are correct. You were not here then but I know from the gossip of the barracks how friendly you were with Monsieur du Jonca."

De Launay was afraid and he had good reason, even I shivered as D'Estivet listed the names of all who had guarded Iron Mask. All had died within seven years of their prisoner. De Launay, clearly agitated, came closer.

"Messieurs," he murmured. "I cannot speak now but perhaps in an hour's time I will meet you in the Café Procope. It's to the left of the surgeon's shop, which stands to the right of the San Antoine gate of the Bastille. I promise to be there. I may bring someone else."

We had no choice and did as the fellow asked. We found the Café Procope easily enough and whiled away the time drinking large bowls of black, sweetened coffee. God knows how I love the smell, so sweet on a clear day's air and sweeter still when mingled with the smell of tobacco from a clay pipe.

I would have questioned D'Estivet on the list of names of all the masked prisoner's gaolers who had died, but

D'Estivet was rather agitated. He kept taking out his fob watch and whispering to Maurepas, who murmured how all would be well and that we had all the evening before us.

At last De Launay arrived: his companion was an old man in a black, faded suit, liberally spotted with the vestiges of a thousand meals. His hose was dirty and darned, his shoes battered out of shape while his wig was like a rusty mess of wire, too large for the thin head and narrow face. De Launay apologised profusely for his lateness and introduced his companion, an Englishman, Doctor Nelaton. I saw D'Estivet dip his hand in the dregs of the coffee and make a strange sign on the table, a squat, square cross with a crown at the top. I noticed it because he had drawn the same sketch when we met, that first evening in the Louvre Palace. Now he repeated the sign, glancing at both De Launay and Nelaton as if expecting some reaction but they, like me, totally ignored it. D'Estivet smiled to himself and smoothed the sign out with his fingers as if it were nothing but an absent-minded gesture.

De Launay began by explaining how Doctor Nelaton used to attend prisoners in the Bastille, including the one commonly termed either the 'Ancient Prisoner' or 'The Mask'. Nelaton, eyes half closed, told us what he knew in a reedy, sing-song voice as if relating a story he had told a thousand times.

"I was chief apprentice in a surgeon's shop," he explained, "and was brought in to bleed a prisoner. The governor of the Bastille, Saint-Mars himself, took me up to his chamber in one of the towers. I learnt from Saint-Mars' whispered conversation with the guard that this man was special, he called him the 'Ancient Prisoner'. Anyway," Nelaton said, "when I entered the room, my patient was sitting on a stool, not masked though his head and face was completely enveloped in a towel which was knotted behind his neck."

"Did he say anything?" Maurepas asked.

"He complained of violent pains in the head," Nelaton replied. "So I fastened the leeches and bled him quite copiously. Oh," the doctor added triumphantly, "his voice was low, clear, courtly but he spoke with a definite English accent."

"An English accent!" I exclaimed.

Nelaton narrowed his eyes at me.

"I know of Monsieur Maurepas and Captain D'Estivet," he said. "But who are you?"

"An English archivist," I lied. "A keeper of precious manuscripts, now living in France. I am in the personal service of the Regent."

Nelaton smiled, which turned his face even more into a death-mask.

"Ah, well, fellow countryman, the man I bled was one of ours. He had an English accent."

"Any distinguishing marks?" D'Estivet asked.

"Yes, his skin was brown, tanned by the sun, and he was remarkably well built."

Maurepas nodded and D'Estivet shifted on the bench. He plainly disliked Nelaton and there were no further questions until Maurepas had ordered more bowls of coffee and small, thimbleful-sized glasses of cognac.

"And you, Lieutenant De Launay?" D'Estivet asked as if speaking to one of his own subalterns. "What can you tell us about the prisoner?"

The soldier swilled the liquid around the brandy glass before swallowing it in one gulp.

"I knew du Jonca, Saint-Mars' lieutenant of the Bastille. He told me how the masked prisoner arrived at three o'clock on the afternoon of Thursday, 18th September 1698. He was concealed and was under orders not to speak to anyone or tell anyone his name. He was put in the Basiniére Tower where Saint-Mars himself looked after him until he died on the 19th

November 1703, rather suddenly about ten in the evening. His confession was heard by the chaplain, Monsieur Giraut. He died a few minutes after that and was buried the following day."

"On the death certificate," Maurepas commented, "his name was given as Marciel, whereas I have seen it copied Marchiele. Does that name mean anything to you?"

De Launay shook his head.

"Nothing. I have never heard such a name." He took us all in with one sly glance. "But that should mean little," he smiled. "The prisoner's age is given as forty-five but that is ridiculous. I have seen the original, even the two witnesses, Rosarges and Reilhe, deliberately mis-spelt their own names."

"Do you have anything to add?" D'Estivet asked.

"No."

De Launay looked at Nelaton, now guzzling his bowl of coffee.

"Nor do I think anyone will." he

continued. "After the masked prisoner's death, or so du Jonca told me, Saint-Mars ordered everything connected with the prisoner to be burnt; linen, clothes, mattress and blankets, books, any possessions. Even the walls of the prison were scraped and whitewashed. The tiles pulled up off the floor and new ones laid for fear he might have left some evidence of his identity." De Launay drained his coffee bowl. "Gentlemen, I have told you all I know. Like you, to my dying day, I will wonder who the masked prisoner was!"

After Maurepas had impressed upon both men the need for secrecy and confidentiality, we left the Café Procope. I thought we would go back to the Louvre but Maurepas took me by the wrist, smiled and said he would like me to join them for supper at his own house. We left the Faubourg Saint Antoine and followed the road which runs parallel to the Seine, turning right, down to the Opéra. Behind this lay a small cul-de-sac; the houses here were pleasant, their plaster and timber fronts painted pink, black or white. The shutters were open and polished, the horn glass in each window shining like a jewel. Flower baskets hung from hooks in front of doors or packed on to the broad windowsills of each floor. Even the small cobbled street seemed to glow with a fresh brightness after the sudden spring showers.

I was both gratified and intrigued by Maurepas' hospitality. At first I had considered Maurepas and D'Estivet colleagues, business acquaintances, but the way they talked and conversed, I realised they were firm allies and I wondered what other ties bound them together. As soon as the smart front door of Maurepas' house swung open, I knew the reason; Marie, Maurepas' daughter and only child, stood there as beautiful as any courtly lady; dark, blood-red hair framed a white oval face, perfectly formed lips, a generous mouth, a retroussé nose and large, widespaced, sea-green eyes. Her very severity of dress, a dark blue velvet embroidered with brocade, only emphasized her outstanding beauty. She smiled at her father and D'Estivet but frowned at me as if I was not welcome. Maurepas laughingly embraced and kissed her. D'Estivet took her hand in his, brushing it softly with his lips, his cold, dead eyes now alive with joy in the presence of this lovely girl. Marie made a strange sound with her mouth and gesticulated at her father, making signs with her fingers and hands, courtly and deftly, as any professional dancer. Maurepas grinned and clumsily made the same signs back.

"Marie," he said slowly and I watched the girl study his lips. "This is Ralph Croft. He is English and," he cracked the usual joke common amongst the French, "this goddam, beef-eater has no tail!" He turned to me. "Ralph, my daughter, Marie."

I clicked my heels and bowed. Marie

copied me so aptly that both her father and D'Estivet burst into loud peals of laughter. Maurepas took me by the arm.

"Come in Croft! I'll explain later."

I was about to cross the threshold when a sound from the street made me turn quickly and I went back into the cold evening air. Since leaving the Café Procope I was sure we were being followed. I thought I caught a glimpse of a man, standing in the darkness in the far corner of the square. I stared again but could see nothing so I dismissed it and re-entered the house, ignoring D'Estivet's and Maurepas' surprised glances.

The chief archivist's home was a splendid building: polished oak floor and wainscoting, thick, rich, woollen carpets; portraits, framed in dark oak, most of them based on Roman themes. There were also plaster busts on small marble columns; the heads of the Gracchi, Demosthenes, Cicero and Brutus.

"All the great orators!" Maurepas announced expansively. "Great orators who fought against tyrants!"

I thought it was a startling statement coming from a man in the employ of princes but I kept my mouth shut. I was ushered into the luxurious dining-room lit by rows of tall, white candles where Maurepas' servants had prepared a veritable banquet for us. The fire had been lit; the flames were roaring under the great hooded mantelpiece and the table was covered by a cream, silk cloth which shimmered like a sea of glass. Six three-branched candelabra had been placed down the centre of the table. Next to each of these, a small vase of spring flowers, silver cruets and tall, thin Venetian glassware. Maurepas and his daughter sat at each end of the table with D'Estivet and me facing each other. The Archivist said Grace and ordered the meal to be served immediately. Oh, it was the best I had ever eaten! In heaven God's cooks must be French! There was ham stuffed with cloves, seasoned with cinnamon and sprinkled with sugar; filet of venison with truffle partridge, beef (a concession for me, an Englishman, Maurepas joked) flavoured with marjoram and surrounded with slices of pheasant, sprinkled with tarragon and violets, and finally capon, specially cooked and stuffed with fresh oysters. A jug of claret was passed round as Maurepas commented and introduced each dish. I needed little invitation for I was ravenous. I let Maurepas chatter as I only had eyes for his beautiful, enigmatic daughter.

"You seem to be intrigued by Marie," Maurepas announced proudly. "Most men are, are they not, D'Estivet?"

The soldier shrugged, embarrassed.

"Marie is deaf and dumb," Maurepas continued quietly, "and has been since birth. Her mother, my poor wife, died in childbirth, not," he smiled wanly, "that Marie caused her death." His eyes took on a far-away expression. "More due to circumstances," he murmured, "beyond anyone's control. My wife's parents were Huguenots, what you English call Protestants. You know what happened in France? Louis XIV may have been the Sun King to Catholics but to the Huguenots he was nothing but a devil: he repealed the edicts of toleration brought in by his father and thousands of Huguenots were imprisoned, Marie's grandparents amongst them." Maurepas twisted a ring around on his finger. "Shortly before my wife gave birth, both her parents died of gaol fever. I believe my wife died of shock."

The room fell silent except for the crackling of the logs on the fire. I stared at this strange girl, sad for her, sad for her mother, for her grandparents, sad for myself, sad for the loss of Abigail, sad that I was there and not in my own house. I felt the anger, loosened by the rich claret, break free and seep bitterly into my soul. I was a prisoner in a foreign country amongst strangers whom I knew little about. Maurepas must have caught my mood.

"You are probably fascinated," he remarked, "by the sign language Marie uses. A German professor taught her it. Marie taught me and then D'Estivet."

"I would like to learn it too," I said.

The girl smiled dazzlingly, her eyes dancing with laughter which made me blush and drew dark looks from D'Estivet.

"And who is your God, Croft?" Maurepas asked, quickly diverting the conversation at D'Estivet's sudden display of jealousy.

"I don't know," I replied. "In France He's French and Catholic. Across the water He's English and Protestant. My God and I don't have a relationship. I stopped talking to him when He stopped talking to me."

Both Maurepas and D'Estivet laughed. Marie smiled and I also realised she could lip-read.

"And princes?" D'Estivet said slowly. "Do you believe in them?"

"'Be not like the pagans,'" I intoned quoting scripture. "'Whose great men liked to lord it over them.'"

Maurepas and D'Estivet again chuckled. Marie rose and, as she served coffee and large glasses of brandy, I brought the conversation back to what we had learnt so far about the prisoner in the mask. I half suspected that Maurepas and D'Estivet had brought me back to get me drunk and loosen my tongue. However, I am West Country born, raised on dark, heavy cider which would fell a bullock; the claret and brandy, though heady, had not turned my wits. I lucidly listed the facts we had established. First, the prisoner had been hidden away for about thirty years in prisons throughout France before being brought back to the Bastille five years before he died. Secondly, he had been told not to give his name or speak to anyone. Thirdly, he was in the constant care of one gaoler, Saint Mars. Fourthly, the prisoner wore a mask, perhaps of iron, certainly of velvet. He was tall and well built, his skin darkened by the sun, he spoke French with an English accent and suffered from violent headaches. Finally, the name and age given on the prisoner's death certificate had been deliberately false. After his death his corpse had been decapitated, the coffin apparently strewn with acid whilst his cell had been thoroughly cleansed of any evidence of his true name and identity.

"But who?" I asked. "Who was this man?"

Marie, who had rejoined us at the head of the table, made urgent signs with her lovely, long fingers. Maurepas turned to me.

"My daughter says 'Why was he a prisoner so long? Why didn't the old king just kill him? After all, life is so cheap.'"

None of us could answer her questions. More coffee was served. I refused extra brandy for I felt tired and sleepy. Maurepas was now lost in his own thoughts; Marie and D'Estivet were smiling at each other like long-separated lovers and I noticed, with a pang of jealousy, how skilful he was in communicating with her through the sign language. I rose to go and took my leave of Marie and D'Estivet. Maurepas accompanied me to the door. He opened it and walked out with me into the darkness.

"You could flee, Ralph," he said. "You could run now."

"Where to?" I shrugged. "What is the use of the running if the race never ends?"

The archivist smiled.

"You are right, Ralph. We live in dangerous times. Tomorrow we will go through the records. Let us search out this secret and all will be well for you, for the Regent, for all of us."

Maurepas shook my hand. I heard the door close behind him and I walked back across the square. I thought of Marie and envied D'Estivet's friendship with her. I idly wondered whether I should flee but found little desire for it. For the moment I was safe, secure and intrigued by this mystery. I stopped as I heard a sound behind me and smiled. Yes, I thought, one day all these secrets will be revealed, even the identity of the man following me so stealthily in the darkness.

4

THE next morning, under the supervision of Maurepas and D'Estivet, I began a thorough search of the official records. Maurepas was as pleasant as ever but D'Estivet was rather cool, he must have seen me as a rival for the heart of Marie. All I could do was smile at him and secretly wonder when I would meet Marie again, for her face and silent beauty haunted me.

Maurepas proved to be a hard taskmaster, he explained how the prisoner had been under the direct control of the Minister of War. There were three such ministers under Louis XIV; Louvois, who died in 1691, his son Barbezieux until 1698, and Chamillart until the prisoner's death in 1703. Once again I was chilled to realise how two of these, Louvois and Barbezieux, had died suddenly and mysteriously. I pointed this out to Maurepas. He shrugged and muttered something about the prisoner bringing ill-fortune to those around him.

"But, look," he said, placing two great, leather-bound volumes on the table in front of me. "A summary of any letter or document sent regarding the prisoner would either be recorded in the minute book of the Ministry of War or the royal register. It is simply a task of going through both records and building up a picture of the official documents regarding our prisoner."

He and D'Estivet then left me to it. I shall not recount the hours and days I spent on this task. The job was arduous for I had to ensure that every entry, every record was genuine and had not been tampered with. Naturally, I found a few that were, names or dates crossed out, simply blanks in the documents. The task was made no easier by the fact that Louis XIV and his ministers sent out literally hundreds of letters a week. I felt like a miner digging in the dark, moving tons of earth and dross to find one gem. Eventually, after five hard days under my taskmasters, I was able to draw up a memorandum. I still have a copy because I was cunning enough to make a fair record of all I wrote. It reads as follows:

"Memorandum drawn up by Ralph Croft, completed and sealed on Friday, April 19th 1719. I have studied both the royal register and the minute book of the Ministry of War. I understand that all documents concerning the prisoner should have been recorded here. I am now able, having cleared all other impedimenta, to describe the documentation regarding the masked man as follows. First, it would appear that the prisoner's gaoler, Etienne Saint-Mars, was the sword name of Benigne D'Auvergne, assumed by him when he entered the army as a cadet in 1638. He was under the guardianship of his uncle, who managed to buy him a place in the first company of the

King's Musketeers. He was promoted to Corporal in 1660 and Serjeant in 1664. In the December of that year his superior officer, the famous swordsman and musketeer, Captain D'Artagnan, recommended that he be made Governor of the State Prison of Saint Pignerol in the Piedmontese Hills twenty-three miles south-west of Turin. His appointment coincided with the incarceration of Nicholas Fouquet, once Chief Minister of Finance under Louis XIV, who fell from office in 1661 though he was not brought to trial and sentenced to life imprisonment until 1664.

"Fouquet was Saint-Mars' only prisoner until 1669 when Saint-Mars was ordered to prepare a high-security cell at Pignerol for a secret prisoner who was to be furnished with nothing except the simple necessities of life — 'because he is only a valet'. This prisoner, undoubtedly the man in the iron mask, was to be threatened with death if he spoke about anything but his basic needs. He was to have contact with no one except Saint-Mars himself. (There seems to be a contradiction here: on the one hand the prisoner is only a valet but the security precautions taken must surely make him the most expensive valet in the history of France.) A special cell was built for him, so important was he that King Louis sent Poupart, his own Minister of Fortifications, to Pignerol to view the place. The following year the Minister of War himself, Louvois, together with the greatest military engineer France has known, Vauban, also went to Pignerol to check security arrangements.

"There also seems to be confusion over the secret prisoner's arrest. Saint-Mars was told to prepare these new security arrangements at Pignerol on the 19th July 1669 but it was not until 28th July of the same year, that the King himself issued an arrest warrant to a Serjeant Major Vauroy to seize a man in Dunkirk and deliver him to Pignerol and the custody of Saint-Mars. Once again the enigma is here: a valet, but someone who has to be securely locked away: a cell is prepared for him but the actual arrest warrant is not issued until nine days later.

"Other riddles ensue: in 1670 Saint-Mars has another prisoner sent to him, the Captain of the King's own bodyguards, the Comte de Lauzun. Accordingly, Saint-Mars had three important prisoners: Nicholas Fouquet (the ex-Minister of Finance), our own masked prisoner and Lauzon. Fouquet is allowed to talk to the masked prisoner but no one else is permitted access to him. Ten years after the masked prisoner's arrest, Louvois actually writes to Fouquet in prison. 'You will have gathered from Saint-Mars about the precautions the King wants implemented to hinder our secret prisoner from talking to anyone except yourself. His Majesty expects you to give great care to this matter because you know how important it is that no one has knowledge of *what he knows.'* A month later the Minister of War writes to Saint-Mars to warn him that the secret prisoner does not talk to anyone in private. The only conclusion I can draw from all of this is that the ex-Minister of France, Fouquet, must have known the real identity of the prisoner. Could this knowledge be the real reason why Fouquet fell from power so dramatically in 1661?

"In 1680 Fouquet died in rather mysterious circumstances but it then appears that Fouquet's valet, La Rivière, had also learnt the secret of the man in the iron mask. On the 8th April 1680, Louvois writes again to Saint-Mars: because La Rivière knows what he does, the poor man is to be imprisoned for life whilst Saint-Mars is to circulate the rumour that both La Rivière and the secret prisoner have been released. The following year, 1681, Saint-Mars transported these two prisoners (La Rivière and the masked man) to the Fortress of Les Exiles and they were taken there in a litter. In 1687 La

Rivière, suffering from dropsy, died and Saint-Mars and his secret prisoner were now moved to the Fortress of Sainte Marguerite.

"A local spy witnessed this transfer and writes, 'No one knows who he is. He is forbidden to speak his name and he is to be shot immediately if he should pronounce it. He was transported in a sedan chair with a steel mask on his face.' In 1691 Barbézieux became Minister of War in succession to his father, Louvois, and in 1696 Saint-Mars has to give him a description of the incredible security precautions taken with the prisoner. Saint-Mars' reply, printed in full in the minute book, is dated 6th January 1696.

"'You asked me to give you details of the arrangements made when I am absent or too ill for the day-to-day visits regarding the ancient prisoner who is in my charge. My two lieutenants feed the prisoner at regular times, as I do. The senior lieutenant takes the keys to the cell of the ancient prisoner and opens all three doors which gives access to the inter-connecting chambers. He then goes to the prisoner who will hand over all the dishes and plates he has used. The senior lieutenant takes these out and hands them over to one of my serjeants, who places them on a table. It is the duty of the other lieutenant to inspect these and anything else going in and out of the cell and to check that there is nothing written on the plates. After this, an inspection is made inside and under the bed and of everything else and this includes the bars of the window, even the privy! This inspection of the cell is made every day and often a body search is included. Then, when the prisoner has been asked in a civil fashion if he needs anything, the doors are closed and locked. All his linen is changed twice a week, carefully counted and inspected on its collection and return, as prisoners of consequence have been known either to write on these or bribe the washerwoman. All such linen is soaked immediately and, when it is clean and half dry, a servant brings it to my apartments where it is ironed and folded in the presence of one my lieutenants. The laundry is then locked in a strong box until handed over to the prisoner himself. Candles are also checked, these are specially purchased from Turin. As a final security precaution, we also visit the prisoner unexpectedly at all hours, both day and night.'

"Finally, in March 1698 Saint-Mars was appointed Governor of the Bastille. On the 15th June of that year he was ordered to travel to Paris 'and take with you, in all security, your ancient prisoner', the term now used for the masked man. On the 19th July that year one final letter is written; the relevant minute reads as follows: 'The King approves that you should leave the Isles of Sainte Marguerite to go to the Bastille with your ancient prisoner, taking all precautions to prevent his being seen or recognised by anyone. You can write in advance to His

Majesty's Lieutenant at that fortress to have a chamber ready so as to be able to place your prisoner in it on your arrival.'

"One final postscript concerns not so much the prisoner but Saint-Mars himself. He was nothing but a peasant, a mere corporal, yet by the time he moved to the Bastille he was an extremely rich man. In pounds sterling he must have been earning something like £35,000 a year. He also received lump sums from Louvois, £25,000 in 1677, almost £15,000 two years later. Saint-Mars received three titles and the governorship of at least half a dozen towns and castles. True, he must have been as much a prisoner as the masked man himself but he was well paid for it. To conclude, what we know of the prisoner is as follows:

"He was tall, spoke with an English accent and was arrested by a sergeant-major Vauroy at Dunkirk in 1669 and transferred to Pignerol prison. He was moved to two other prisons before being transferred to the Bastille. He was allowed to speak to no one. He was not to tell anyone his real name (a matter I will come to in a while), if he attempted to do so he would be shot immediately. He was only a valet yet special cells were constructed for him at Pignerol, which were inspected by the Minister of War himself, and at Sainte Marguerite where the new cell cost over seven thousand pounds sterling. His secret was known to the disgraced Minister of Finance, Fouquet, and even thirty years after the masked man's capture his face was still being hidden behind a mask. So who was he? Apparently, his name meant something and people looking at his face might draw certain conclusions. So what was his name? In the minute books it has been carefully erased but, by using chemicals on one document, I have established that the prisoner's first name was Eustace and his surname begins with D. We need to find the original letters before we obtain the name in full and even then our hunt might only be beginning."

Both my companions were delighted with my work. Maurepas hugged me and D'Estivet shook my hand. They toasted my success in cup after cup of wine. I hoped for a second invitation to Maurepas' home and was enchanted to receive it. Not as grand an occasion as the last time but seemly enough, chilled wine and cold meats in the small orchard behind the house. Marie looked as beautiful as ever, dressed in a dark red dress, her head covered with a white gauze veil. She reminded me of a picture of the Madonna I had seen in stained glass in Notre Dame. This time I did not care for D'Estivet or his feelings but drew the girl into teaching me some of the sign language she used. I was an avid and keen pupil. God has blessed me with a sharp brain and a sound memory and, unknown to D'Estivet and Maurepas, I made excellent progress in it. I am glad for it later saved my life.

I was also intrigued by what Maurepas

and D'Estivet had been doing whilst I was working on the manuscript and I was pleased to find they had not met with as much success as myself. Maurepas had journeyed down to the Chateau Palteau in an attempt to seize the family papers of Saint-Mars but, strangely enough, these were no longer in existence, being either destroyed or lost. D'Estivet had visited the vagabond underworld of Paris in an unsuccessful attempt to discover prisoners, men who had been in the Bastille at the same time as the masked man. However, he had achieved nothing but only received dark looks and threats. Maurepas shrugged as they both confessed their failure.

"So, Ralph, we are pleased with you. We know this masked man must surely have been someone very important. We know about the security precautions taken. We know his gaoler was bribed with money and honours. We know the man's face was in itself a direct threat to the crown and that his first name was Eustace. Yet," he concluded, "if it was, why was Marciel written on the death certificate?"

I shook my head.

"I can't answer that though I have a feeling that the word 'Marciel' will eventually solve the riddles."

"What riddles?" Maurepas asked.

"Well, for decades the reason and manner of this man's capture were hidden away. The Ministry of War went to great efforts to hide what really happened. I mean, the whole business of the arrest, a cell is prepared but only nine days later is the actual arrest warrant issued and to whom? A sergeant major in Dunkirk called Vauroy is told to act secretly, he is not even to inform his superiors. But how was Vauroy supposed to recognise this Eustace? Would you send a letter to someone in London telling him to arrest John Brown? There are many men with that name. You would need a detailed description of his appearance, clothes, etc., but this was not given. Finally, there is the business of Matteoli!"

"Ah!"

I saw Maurepas' eyes widen a little.

"What do you know," he asked, "of Matteoli?"

D'Estivet now put his cup down and watched me intently.

"Why all the surprise?" I asked.

"Because," Maurepas grinned, "some people believe that Matteoli is the masked prisoner because his name sounds like Marciel."

"What was his crime?" I asked.

"He offered to sell an Italian fortress to King Louis XIV but then tried to embezzle the French King's money. Why," Maurepas asked, "what do you know?"

"According to the Ministry of War minutes," I replied, "Matteoli was a very important prisoner though he cannot be our man. First, he was not arrested until 1679 and then on the Franco-Italian border, not at Dunkirk. Secondly, he was given a prison name, Lestang, but no reference is made to his being masked. Thirdly, according to Louvois, Matteoli was insane by 1680, while our prisoner appears to have kept his wits. Finally, Matteoli's crime was well known whilst every attempt was made to hide the identity and deeds of the masked prisoner."

Maurepas gave a deep sigh and shifted uneasily in his chair. He strummed his lip with his finger, idly watching a bird jab the soil with its cruel beak.

"I have tried another method," he said slowly. "I have searched amongst the court records for any notable who may have disappeared suddenly in the years 1668 and 1669. The only person I can discover is the Grand Admiral of France, the Duke of Beaufort." Maurepas rubbed the side of his face and yawned. "Beaufort was a troublemaker. He moved from one plot to another like flies do to heaps of shit. He was an enemy of Louis XIV's mother, Queen Anne, but managed to gain the King's favour and led an expedition against the Turks in Crete. Beaufort may have been a fool but he was a brave one. He led a frontal assault on the Turkish camp, the attack was unsuccessful until a Turkish ammunition dump, hit by a chance bullet, exploded killing many French. The Turks launched a counterattack. The French were driven back and Beaufort disappeared. It may well be that the Turks captured him and handed him back to Louis who clapped him in gaol." Maurepas stopped and waved a hand at me. "I know my theory is as full of holes as a fisherman's net. Why should the Turks hand Beaufort over? Why should Louis bring a troublemaker back to France and hide him away? Why call him Eustace?" Maurepas drained his wine glass. "It's the best I can do for there's no one else who mysteriously disappeared in 1669, 1670 or 1671." He sighed. "It's all a great mystery." He stood up. "But come, Ralph, I will walk you back to the Louvre. D'Estivet, you will join us?"

I could see the soldier would have much preferred to sit and flirt with Marie, but we all made our adieux. I was secretly gratified by the flattering smile Marie bestowed on me and I wondered if D'Estivet's hold on his young lady's heart was as secure as he thought it was. We walked back most of the way in silence. I kept thinking of Marie, D'Estivet was sulking beside me whereas Maurepas was lost in his own thoughts. Just before we reached the Louvre Maurepas stopped and faced us both.

"Ralph, I wish you would do me a favour for we place great trust in you. D'Estivet tried to talk to people, men who had been imprisoned in the Bastille. We thought he would find them in the Faubourg Saint-Antoine." Maurepas smiled. "But the underworld of Paris is more murky than we thought. We are looking for one particular man. A radical, a rogue though one who may know something. He is called Constantine de Renneville. He is still wanted by the police because of his scurrilous writings about Louis XIV, as well as certain ladies of the Versailles court. We want you to re-enter the Faubourg Saint-Antoine, find him, discover all he knows and bring this information back."

D'Estivet was about to protest but Maurepas silenced him with a gesture of his hand.

"Captain," he said slowly, "you have tried your best. Ralph knows the streets, more importantly, he knows the people who live there."

"But you wonder whether I will come back?"

"Exactly," Maurepas replied. "But we trust you."

"And, if we are wrong," D'Estivet broke in heartily, "if our trust is betrayed," he turned, his face only a few inches away from mine, "I promise you this, Croft, I will hunt you down and kill you!"

D'Estivet suddenly stepped back and, in a flashing arc of steel, drew his sword.

I have seen good street brawlers, bully boys, professional duellists but none could equal his display of swordmanship. Time and again, he skipped backwards and forwards, the point of his sword only a few inches away from my chest or face. The weapon was like a magic wand, turning, twisting, twinkling in the faint sunlight so fast, so deadly, all I saw was a flash of steel and D'Estivet's quick movements. His face remained impassive, his cold, dead eyes never left mine. Then he stopped as quickly as he had begun and sheathed his sword.

"I think," Maurepas commented drily, "that Ralph understands your message, Captain!"

D'Estivet spun on his heel and strode away whilst Maurepas urged that I begin my work in the Faubourg Saint-Antoine immediately. He and D'Estivet would try to obtain the original letters and so discover the full name of the masked prisoner. I watched them both walk away, arms linked, and heard D'Estivet laugh softly at something

Maurepas said. I made one resolve, watching the archivist and the killer; if D'Estivet turned openly hostile, I would slay him before his hand ever touched his sword.

I walked back through the crowds thronging about the palace. The royal guard allowed me through for they now accepted me as another member of the huge palace household. I went straight up to my chamber, wanting to sleep, for I felt tired after the walk and the cups of heavy wine I had drunk at Maurepas' house. I opened the door of my chamber and met the Abbé Fleury for the first time. He sat perched on my bed; his thin, sallow face a mask of contentment, his small, bright eyes enjoying my consternation.

"Before you ask who I am," he began, "my name is Abbé Fleury. I am a priest and personal tutor to his young Majesty Louis XV." He got up and gathered his cloak tightly about him. "I still think it's cold," he said, "despite the sun." He looked around.

"Your chamber is not the warmest room in the palace."

"Monsieur Abbé," I replied, "I thank you for your concern but I would like to know why a stranger, no matter how important he may be, had my chamber unlocked and sits waiting for me as if I am some lackey returning from an errand!"

I took my own cloak off and threw it on the bed.

"I suppose," I contintued. "You have already looked around for documents, papers, etc."

The abbé smiled, displaying a row of white, polished teeth which he ground together as if trying to hide his own amusement at my discomfiture. He shot one bony, thin hand towards me, jabbing at the air with his finger.

"I heard you were sharp, Monsieur Croft, but beware you do not cut yourself!"

I slumped down on the bed and looked up at the ceiling, not caring whether the fellow stood or sat.

"What do you mean?" I asked.

"You know what I mean. The task you are involved with. Knowledge is a very dangerous thing, Englishman. What happens if you learn more than you should? Do you think you are going to be allowed to walk away?"

He stood over me, his face grave and concerned.

"I suppose you have already thought of that, Croft. I have come to warn you to be careful. Trust me when I tell you that nothing is what it seems to be, and that certainly applies to your two friends, Monsieur Maurepas and Captain D'Estivet!"

Abbé Fleury touched me gently on the cheek.

"If danger threatens, and it certainly will, come to me. Anyone in the palace will tell you where I am."

I looked at him and closed my eyes as if falling asleep. I heard the door open and close and, for the first time since I had been brought to the Louvre, I was genuinely frightened.

5

THE next morning I rose early, donned my oldest clothes, and walked into the Faubourg Saint-Antoine. London has its Alsatia, its Southwark slums, but nothing can equal the degradation and poverty of that quarter in Paris. The houses are huddled together; dingy dwellings, two, three stories high. Some are hundreds of years old because, unlike London, there has been no great, cleansing fire. The streets are really tunnels, filth-strewn and reeking as they run in haphazard fashion; the sky is blocked out by the upper stories of the houses on either side, in some places hardly an arm's length separates them. A veritable thieves' kitchen where children run naked, enjoying a few months of happiness before contracting some deadly disease, being injured in an accident or being employed by their parents in some illegal activity. First, I went to Monfaucon for, as on every morning, some felon was being executed; strapped across the hub of the great wheel, he would be slowly turned as red masked executioners smashed his arms and legs. That particular morning was no different: the man about to be executed had attempted a jewel robbery in the Rue St Everard, killing two people before being apprehended.

I do not like public executions, not even my own, and I remembered that only the intervention of the Regent had saved me from ending my days screaming as my limbs were smashed by iron bars. I also find the baying of the mob diabolic, such occasions attract the scum and the filth of the city. I was looking for a rogue, a King of the Vagabonds who controlled such rogues and criminals as ruthlessly as any diligent officer would a troop of soldiers. I arrived to hear the condemned man's last screams and faint moans. I hurriedly gazed across the crowd, looking for this self-styled lord of the underworld. He always attended such occasions, being the only time he ever came out in public. At last, amongst a crowd at the foot of the scaffold, I glimpsed him; a tall man, with blond hair and the face of a preacher, yet this fellow commanded assassins and murderers who would cut a child's throat without turning a hair. Dressed completely in black, he looked like a Calvinist preacher, even down to his steeple hat with its white head-band. Once I had caught sight of my quarry. I had no difficulty following him from the execution ground back into the depths of the Faubourg Saint-Antoine. Captain Villon (or so he calls himself) was re-entering his kingdom, surrounded by his protectors: a prince who rules the Faubourg and every pimp, thief and robber is his subject.

Villon walked through the streets like a king; usually tradesmen would come out shouting, "Pears and Pippins!"

"Flat Brooms!" "Sweets!" but, when Villon passed, they fell silent and drew away. Deeper into the darkness he went, past a half-burnt-out church. I nearly lost him there for I was set upon by the sellers of second-hand clothes who leapt out at me from behind their makeshift stalls to pull at my hand, grip my shoulders or shout in my ear. I shrugged them off, running after Villon as he crossed a small square, where evil-looking men stood by barrows piled high with nuts, gingerbread, oranges and oysters. Old crones in straw hats or flat caps offered hose, nightcaps and plum puddings for sale. You can buy anything there from a pair of whale-bone stays or a toothbrush to a patch box or a squirrel's cage: clothes, hats, trinkets, toys, gloves, fans, silk stockings and bottles of perfume stacked high, available for a few sous for anyone to purchase. Most of the merchandise is stolen, brought to such illegal market places where no provost of police or government agent could interfere.

Villon crossed a few more filthy streets into the heart of the Faubourg, not stopping until he came to a tavern 'The Devil's Cauldron', a small, dingy, two-storied affair. Inside, the place was low-timbered with rushes on the floor, in one far corner a row of barrels and in the centre a huge hearth where a fire always burns, even in the height of summer. As I came through the doorway, Villon had crossed to this, sitting down in a high-backed chair like a king assuming his throne so he could watch the entire room fill with every type of villain in Paris. Around him his minions took their places as if preparing for some macabre Last Supper, crouched about him like fawning dogs at their master's feet. The landlord ran up, offering the best ale and food the inn could provide and within a twinkling of an eye, a table had been laid and prepared before Villon. Huge platters of boiled meat garnished with vegetables and deep broad cups of red wine were served.

I sat well away, watching this macabre scene before summoning the landlord. I ordered wine and asked the fellow to present my compliments to Captain Villon for I, Ralph Croft alias Scaramac, wished to have words with him. The landlord recognised me for, although the Faubourg Saint-Antoine is thronged with people, a forger or counterfeit man like myself is well known to all. From his eyes I could see that the accepted view was that I should either be dead or forgotten, locked away in some prison. He looked as if he was going to refuse so I slipped him some silver. The landlord nodded and shuffled across the room like a spider, bowing and scraping as he delivered the message. A number of the Master Criminal's retainers stared across at me but Villon kept on eating and my heart sank. Was he going to refuse to talk to me? Nevertheless, being obstinate, I decided I would stay there until he acceded to my request. After a while, Villon stopped eating, looked up and indicated imperiously that I should join him. I walked over and, without an invitation, sat down on the corner of a bench and stared at this villain's beatific face; the creamy skin, the soft mouth and the eyes crinkled with laughter lines which even a child would trust. On either side of Villon stood his principal henchmen dressed garishly in a wide range of colours; blues, purples, white cambric shirts, heavy military cloaks, plumed hats, some so huge they hid their wearer's face. I looked at them all and shivered, they all gave off a vapour, an emanation of evil; their faces were lean and scarred, eyes hard and glittering, a pack of rats assembled to plan some dreadful mischief. Villon leaned forward and tapped me on the wrist.

"I know you, Englishman! You're Croft, the forger, the counterfeit man. What do you want with me?"

"Captain," I replied, "here in the Faubourg Saint-Antoine, not even a rat crosses an alleyway without your permission."

The man smiled, accepting the compliment as his due.

"I am looking for a radical," I continued, "an agitator, Constant de Renneville. He is the writer of articles, scurrilous pamphlets against the court. He was also a prisoner in the Bastille."

"Why do you want him?"

"I am involved in a task. I work for some powerful men in the Louvre Palace."

Villon just looked at me.

"Does it concern the Faubourg Saint-Antoine?" he asked.

I just shook my head. Villon grasped my wrists tightly, so hard the bones might crack, but I just stared back, my eyes fixed on his.

"If you are lying, Englishman," the fellow replied, "I will kill you! You understand?"

I nodded and he let me go.

"I can bring de Renneville to you," he said, "but it will have to be here, the landlord will give you a room." He named an exorbitant price and I gasped even though Maurepas had supplied me with enough gold; what worried me was that if it took so much money to hire a room in this hovel what would Villon ask for bringing de Renneville to me? The Vagabond King read my thoughts.

"Like any good customer," he said, "you are worried about the bill. It will cost you nothing. Who is your immediate master?"

"Monsieur Maurepas," I replied.

Villon glanced sideways and muttered something under his breath.

"I know Monsieur Maurepas," he said. "Or, rather, I should say I know of him."

"How?" My curiosity was aroused. "How do you know the Duke of Orleans' archivist?"

"Monsieur Maurepas is sometimes seen in the Faubourg Saint-Antoine, along with his hired killer, Captain D'Estivet. They move in circles we do not like. We have nothing to do with them though we watch their activities."

"Does this mean anything to you?" I asked and, dabbing my finger in a pool of wine on the table, I drew the same strange cross D'Estivet had sketched in the Café Procope. Villon just stretched across and rubbed the drawing out.

"I know what it means," he said. "But I advise you Englishman, to remain blissfully ignorant. In the Faubourg Saint-Antoine, we are concerned with money, not with toppling kings and replacing them with new ones. After all, in your country there is a saying is there not? 'The devil you know is better than the devil you don't know.'" Villon rose. "Now come, Englishman. The landlord will give you the most spacious room in the house, a warm meal, a glass of wine and you shall sleep." He tapped my arm. "Do not worry, you are safe. After all, you are one of us, are you not? Yet, there are things done here that you had best not see. While you sleep I shall send a messenger to Monsieur Maurepas, he can pay the bill; two purses of gold and the names of three men, my men, now lodged in the Montmartre prison. They are due to hang in five days. If they are pardoned, if the gold arrives, you will see Monsieur de Renneville."

"And if not?" I interrupted.

Villon shrugged and flicked a lace-cuffed hand elegantly in the air.

"If not, Englishman, we shall give Monsieur Maurepas something to remember us by and send you packing about your business!"

I confess, that night's slumber was not the easiest. The room was comfortable enough, clean and sparsely furnished, and the meal was fit for a king though the wine was laced with a light sleeping potion. After I had drunk it, I felt unusually drowsy, so fatigued I could only lie on the bed, drifting in and out of sleep, as the noise from the room below drifted up like the baying of tormented souls.

The next morning I rose anxious,

worried lest Maurepas had not replied but, even before I finished dressing, there was a loud knock on the door and Villon walked in. He was accompanied by a tall giant of a man, his leonine grey hair swept back to reveal a high forehead, dark brooding eyes and the strong nose, mouth and chin of a professional pugilist. Villon introduced the newcomer with his usual sardonic courtesy.

"Monsieur de Renneville, Ralph Croft! Both of you are writers," he looked slyly at me, "of sorts! Monsieur Croft has questions to ask you, de Renneville, and you will answer them. Maurepas has paid his price and now, Monsieur de Renneville, you will have to pay yours!" Villon clapped the giant on the shoulder and looked at me. "Monsieur de Renneville is wanted by the Provost and, of course, we hide him. Sirs, I bid you adieu!"

Villon closed the door behind him and I gestured to de Renneville to sit on the room's only chair. I finished dressing, and sat opposite him on the bed. De Renneville closely studied me as if judging me from what I looked like, how I dressed, rather than what I would say. His face would have been strong but it was weakened by a slight cast in one eye and a sardonic smile which curled his mouth and gave a sly, sinister twist to his face.

"Monsieur de Renneville," I began, "I will come quickly to the point. For a while you were a prisoner in the Bastille during the governorship of Saint-Mars. At the same time there was another prisoner there, the one they called the 'Masked Man' or 'Ancient Prisoner'. My masters want what you know about Saint-Mars, his lieutenants and, above all, the prisoner in their charge.

De Renneville stared at me for a while before speaking.

"I was in the Bastille for a number of years," he began slowly. "Saint-Mars was a little weed of a man, a born bureaucrat. When I met him, his eyes were cloudy and dull, full of all the resentments of old age. He wanted to regale people about how important he was and how many men he had killed in duels. Du Jonca, his lieutenant, was not a bad fellow, obliging and honest." De Renneville stirred, becoming more impassioned. "The real bastards were those who worked for Saint-Mars, creatures who had been his servants when he was governor of other prisons."

"Rosarges?" I asked.

"What about him?"

"He signed the death certificate of the masked prisoner!"

"Rosarges was a monster; slightly built and slack-limbed. He had the face of a gargoyle, his clothes were always dirty and filthy and I can't remember a day when he was sober. Oh, I remember Rosarges! Who could forget a face like that, puffed red by booze which had even broken the veins in his nose. He also had a horrible abscess on his lip. He would do anything to keep himself in brandy, whether it be bribes or stealing the clothes off the other prisoners' backs."

"And the surgeon, Reilhe?" I asked. De Renneville laughed.

"Surgeon! More a barber! He couldn't even pull a tooth properly. He was so incompetent he caused more deaths than gaol fever. He liked to ape his superiors and always wore the governor's cast-off clothes and wigs. He was a born sycophant! An opportunist!"

"So both men would lie?"

"They would lie for a sou. They would lie if it would hurt someone. They would not know the truth if it smacked them in their ugly, little faces!"

"And Giraut?" I asked

De Renneville squirmed on the chair.

"Oh, yes, Abbé Giraut, priest and pervert. He wielded tremendous influence over Saint-Mars. The priest was the governor's pet and the governor was the puppet of the priest." De Renneville's face went cold and hard. "Giraut was different: he had more pride, more cunning in his little finger than the rest of them put together. I disliked him as soon as I caught sight of him. He had the face of a parrot. A man so corrupt even Satan himself must have wept at his mischief! He debauched the women prisoners and those who refused his advances he brutalised and raped. A woman friend of mine suffered his attentions. They say she died of a fever but later, when I was released, I found that Giraut had beaten her to death."

"Where are they now?"

De Renneville grinned, displaying teeth as yellow and strong as a horse's.

"You should know that, Englishman," he replied, abruptly changing the conversation. "You can't fool Villon and you can't fool me. I know what you are involved in: you were not saved from the executioner at Monfaucon because of your good looks. You are an expert on forgery, be it paper or pen. You must be involved in some investigation about the masked prisoner. Am I right?"

"You are correct," I replied.

De Renneville leaned closer and waggled one stubby finger in my face.

"Then be careful, Englishman!"

"I have heard that warning before."

"You would do well to heed it! You asked about the masked prisoner's guards. Everyone connected with him is dead: Rosarges, Reilhe, Saint-Mars, Du Jonca and Giraut!" He smiled. "Though Giraut is still hanging about, or so you could say!" De Renneville smirked as if he found something amusing.

"What do you mean by that?" I snapped.

He shrugged.

"I'll show you. After all, your master has paid Villon and Villon's rogues look after me. Anyway, what more can I tell you?"

"Anything you know about the prisoner."

"Oh, I have bits and pieces." He looked away.

"How much?" I asked harshly.

"How much do you have?" he asked.

I undid the belt under my robe, the one with a secret pouch, and emptied every coin onto the bed beside me.

"That much," I said, "and no more."

I watched de Renneville's eyes grow round at the silver and gold coins which gleamed and beckoned from the rough, coarse folds of the blanket.

"First," he said, "there's the nonsense."

"What do you mean?"

"Oh, the usual rubbish that Saint-Mars and his lieutenants gave out about their prisoner. On one occasion I was told that the prisoner was a boy who had insulted both the Jesuits and King Louis. Then there was another story, that the prisoner was freed but I know that's a lie, I once actually saw the man; I was being moved round the Bastille, by mistake I went into a room where the prisoner was but I was pushed out immediately so I did not have much time to see a great deal. I cannot say whether the man's face was covered by a mask but, as soon as the guards saw me coming, they made him turn his back so I could see nothing more than the back of his head."

"What did he look like?"

"He was of about average height and very well built. I thought his hair was black, tied in a queue at the back. I thought this was strange because the prisoner had been in gaol for at least thirty years. It was only afterwards that I realised that what I had seen was not a queue of hair but perhaps the black folds of a mask."

I jingled the coins on the bed beside me.

"Do you have anything else to tell me?"

"I did hear a story," de Renneville continued, "how the grandson of one of Saint-Mars' lieutenants repeated the usual family anecdotes about the prisoner: how he had a white face; his body was large and well built; how he slept little, often pacing his cell at night, and that he was always clothed in brown but given good linen and books." De Renneville looked at the money and licked his lips. "I also heard how Saint-Mars and his officers always remained standing and bare-headed in his presence."

I clinked the money again with my fingers. De Renneville looked at me desperately and I realised that he was as much a puppet as I was. He was in the power of Villon as I was in the hands of Maurepas, D'Estivet and the Regent. I could imagine his existence, writing pamphlets, depending on Villon for protection and begging for every meal. The gold and silver on the bed beside me was probably the most he had ever seen in his long, secretive life.

"What else do you know?" I murmured.

De Renneville took a deep breath.

"Don't lie!" I interjected. "If you lie, I leave!"

"I heard one story," he began slowly, "it came from La Motte, who succeeded to the governorship of

Sainte Marguerite after Saint-Mars and the prisoner left. La Motte had been Saint-Mars' lieutenant there. He told me, when I was gathering information for a pamphlet I intend to write, about a brief exchange between the masked prisoner and Saint-Mars." He rubbed his chin.

"Just repeat," I said, "what you heard."

De Renneville's eyes locked with mine.

"And the money?"

I scooped up a few coins and handed them over.

"I give you that in trust," I said.

De Renneville snatched the money and slipped it into a purse hidden under his threadbare cloak.

"According to La Motte, the masked prisoner had asked — 'Does the King want my life?' and Saint-Mars replied, 'No, my Prince, your life is safe. You have only to allow yourself to be led.'"

I handed across a few more coins.

"You are sure," I asked, "that Saint-Mars called the prisoner a prince?"

"I am!"

"Is there anything else?"

"Yes, one thing more. When Saint-Mars moved his prisoner from Sainte Marguerite to the Bastille he broke his journey at his own private estate at Palteau."

(I knew then that de Renneville was not lying for Maurepas had informed me how the chateau had belonged to Saint-Mars.) "Continue!" I snapped.

"The masked man arrived at the chateau in a litter accompanied by several armed men on horseback. Some peasants, workers on the estate, came to see their absentee lord, Saint-Mars. They stood in the courtyard and looked through the casement windows. The prisoner had his back to them but they noticed how Monsieur Saint-Mars ate with his hat off whilst beside him, on the table, were two loaded pistols. The meal was served by those valets who always accompanied Saint-Mars. Later, the same peasants saw the prisoner cross the courtyard. He wore a black mask so only his teeth and lips could be seen, but he was quite tall and had white hair. They later learnt from a chamber-maid that Saint-Mars actually slept in the same room as the prisoner and never allowed him out of his sight."

De Renneville fell silent, looking hungrily across at the pile of coins beside me. I scooped them up and handed them over.

"They are yours, Monsieur," I said. "You have earned every sou."

De Renneville grinned and shrugged.

"Soon the rest of the world will know it in a pamphlet I intend to publish!"

"Who do you think the prisoner was?" I asked.

De Renneville shook his head.

"I don't know. He was dressed like a valet but they wanted to keep his face hidden and called him Prince."

"Do you believe the story?" I asked.

"That he was a twin brother of King Louis XIV?"

"Nonsense!" the fellow replied. "But I have always felt deep in my heart that if I could learn and publish what this masked prisoner knew, it would shake the very throne of France!" De Renneville stood up.

"Monsieur," I said. "I have one small favour to beg of you."

"You have no more money," de Renneville smirked.

"I know," I replied, "but I beg this of you."

I crossed to a bowl of water, wet the tips of my fingers and on the wall drew the cross sign that I had seen D'Estivet sketch.

"Tell me, Monsieur, what does that mean?"

For the first time since I had met him, de Renneville lost some of his arrogance, his face paled, his huge jaw sagged. There was fear in his eyes.

"What is this?" he murmured. He looked sharply at me. "You are not involved with these?"

"With whom?" I snapped.

"The Templars. You know who they are?"

"No, I do not. All I know is the symbol I have just drawn."

De Renneville punched the wall with his fist.

"It's their sign!" he said. "They are a secret order. No one knows who their Grand Master is. They were founded hundreds of years ago, an order of warrior monks who took vows of chastity, poverty and obedience and fought to protect Jerusalem and the Temple from the Turks. In 1307 Philip IV of France attacked them accusing them of idolatry, sodomy, murder and witchcraft." De Renneville pointed to the small window. "Their Grand Master, Jacques de Molay, was executed, there, in the square in front of Notre Dame Cathedral. Before he died de Molay cursed Philip IV of France and all his descendants. According to history, the

Templars became extinct: in reality, however, they were replaced by a secret organisation which is dedicated to the overthrow of all Philip IV's successors and the restoration of the ancient Merovingian line."

"Which is?" I asked, bemused by this revelation.

"The Dukes of Lorraine," de Renneville answered. "These secret Templars have been most active in their designs. They were responsible for the assassination of Louis XIV's grandfather, Henry IV, and many say they were responsible for the conspiracies both Louis XIII and his son Louis XIV had to face. They are a secret organisation and indulge in witchcraft, sorcery and murder." De Renneville came closer to me. "They are ruthless men, they kill anyone who meddles with them. They exist in small cells, each cell having no more than two or three people, and they are only recognisable by secret signs and ciphers." De Renneville moved to the door. "Ask Villon! No, he won't admit it. So do not ask him. Even he is frightened of them!"

He opened the door and made to leave.

"Monsieur!" I called out. "You said you would show me Abbé Giraut!"

De Renneville came back into the room.

"So I did. So I did," he murmured. "Come with me!"

I followed him down the wooden, rickety stairs. The taproom below was now deserted and being cleaned by a scullion. Two of Villon's rogues loomed up when they saw us and barred our path, both were armed with pistols, daggers and swords.

"You wish to leave?" Captain Villon said as he came quietly behind us. De Renneville turned and spread his hands apologetically.

"I promised to show our guest," he remarked, "the Abbé Giraut. He laughed and Villon also chuckled.

"Then let us show him!" he said and

led us out into the street. The morning seemed fresher and fairer after being locked up in that small room. Villon walked ahead of us jauntily, like a young boy on some errand. He pushed through the stall-sellers and the army of beggars, turning and twisting, he led us along some alleyways and on to a broad avenue which led out of the Faubourg and down to the river Seine. Suddenly he stopped beneath a huge sign depicting a jar and pestle and entered the apothecary's shop. De Renneville followed, grinning from ear to ear like some smug complacent cat. I entered more warily, wondering what was awaiting me. The apothecary, a small Jewish man, dressed in a gown and skull-cap, hurried up but Villon waved him away.

"Abbé Giraut is here!" he said.

I looked around.

"There's no one here!" I said testily.

"Look again, Monsieur!" he repeated. "Abbé Giraut is waiting for you."

The shop was large, shelves lining

the walls were covered with jars and bowls; the whole place reeked of herbs, spices and heavy, musky smells. I stared around, there was no one in sight. Villon came up and gently turned my face to gaze into a far corner.

"Surely, you see Abbé Giraut now?" he smiled.

Of course I did and relished the macabre jest. A skeleton, yellow but complete in every detail, swung dangling from a hook in the ceiling, the cord on which it hung had been passed through a small clasp embedded in the top of the skull. De Renneville went over to it and picked up one bony hand.

"Abbé Giraut, may I present Ralph Croft, an Englishman, who would have loved so much to speak to you."

I gazed at the yellowing bones, the empty eye sockets and the sagging jaw with only a few teeth, black and stumped, remaining. De Renneville turned to me.

"Monsieur Croft, accept my apologies for the joke but Abbé Giraut, like all those who served the masked prisoner, died in mysterious circumstances. He was found on the steps of a church, his throat cut from ear to ear." He tapped the skeleton on its skull. "I claimed the body, I had it boiled so the flesh peeled from the bones, and I gave it to Monsieur the apothecary. It's the only revenge I could get for what Giraut did to my woman." He turned and spat on the swinging skeleton. "You may go, de Renneville!" Villon said quietly.

The radical gave me the sketchiest of bows and slipped silently from the shop. Villon walked over to the apothecary, who was crouched on a stool watching what had happened. He murmured a few words and came back to me.

"You, too, can go, Monsieur Croft! Give my regards to Monsieur Maurepas. Tell him there is no need to pay for the second task." Villon took me by the arm. "You should hurry back. He told me to give you a message."

"What is that?"

"They have found the prisoner's name."

I walked to the door and turned.

"Captain Villon, I thank you, but one last request?"

The man bowed.

"Could you help me escape?"

Villon smiled.

"No, Englishman, I cannot, but do me a favour and I will show you why."

6

THE favour Villon asked was simple enough: warrants and passes to allow people past the city gates and travel unmolested through the countless custom posts which surrounded Paris and blocked the main entrance to every town in France. He provided the parchment, the sealing wax, the different inks and proper quills. In an hour I had made fair copies so that not even the most scrupulous official would detect that they were forgeries. Villon and two of his lieutenants scrutinised them, standing under a window, grunting and murmuring as they held the documents up, examining them for any flaw. At last Villon placed them all in a small leather bag and sauntered back over to me.

"You kept your word, Englishman. Now I shall keep mine." He bowed sardonically towards the door. "Your carriage awaits. Come! Come!" He took a small watch from a pocket in his jerkin, flicking back the pearl-encrusted lid. "We do not have much time!"

Outside the tavern door stood a black carriage, the leather flaps of the window secured tight, its driver swathed in robe and hood. He looked more like a medieval monk than a member of Villon's gang. Beside him sat another fellow similarly attired. I caught the glimpse of pistols and a great blunderbuss lying beneath their feet. The horses, too, were black with silver white plumes standing proudly between their ears.

"A carriage fit for a prince," I murmured.

Villon smiled as he sat down on the leather seat beside me, slamming the door behind him.

"You must know, Englishman, there are kings and there are princes and there are those who rule." He turned and grinned before pulling up his hood. "Or perhaps you have realised that already."

Villon tapped on the carriage roof and the horses pulled away. I could see nothing but I felt the carriage jolting and bumping over the ruts and cobbles, turning violently as it followed the maze of streets and runnels. The sound of market traders, the shrieks of children, the clip-clop of other horses and the thunderous rattle of iron wheels finally died away and the shaking of the carriage and the wine I had drunk lulled me into an uneasy sleep. I woke with a start as the carriage stopped and Villon shook me roughly by the arm. He opened the door: the carriage had pulled into one of the great decaying squares so common in Paris where the houses stand derelict, empty and unused. Villon got out, whispered to the driver to stay and took me into one of the old houses, through a side gate and down a cracked, weed-encrusted path which smelt vilely of urine and decay. He pushed open another gate which led into a huge garden now overgrown by gorse and briars, through this and on to the crossroads of the Latin Quarter, a place of great villainy where students, or those pretending to study, rub shoulders with thieves, vagabonds and men hiding from the law. A gibbet stood there, the irons still bearing the pitch-covered remains of a skeleton, its ghastly face and grinning teeth a grim warning to all who passed. Villon nudged me.

"Not what you think, Englishman. This fellow was not executed for breaking the law. He was a government informer hanged by me."

I was going to make some suitable reply when, from behind the scaffold, there shuffled a dirty old man. He was naked above his waist except for an old leather jerkin which had more holes than leather. His head was wrapped in a filthy cloth and his beard, too, was tied up in a rag. In his scaly hands he carried an old felt cap as a begging-bowl, he stretched this out to me, his mottled face smeared with fresh blood as if he had just fallen into a fit and injured himself. He bobbed and shuffled before me.

"Be off with you!" I roared, more in fright than anger. "Be off and leave us alone!"

The creature slithered closer, his thick red lips, caked with blood, pulled back to reveal the black and yellow stumps of his teeth.

"Be off!" I cried and, looking round, I saw a piece of iron which had fallen from the scaffold and picked it up.

"Enough now, Philippe," Villon interrupted.

Villon's words brought a marvellous transformation in the fellow. He suddenly straightened up, grinned and bowed slightly towards Villon.

"A great actor," Villon commented, looking slyly at me. "Philippe is a gipsy. He is their spy and he will lead us to his people's encampment."

Philippe, despite the paint he had

used to transform himself into a grotesque beggar, was really an accomplished young man who could, in an instant, take on any posture or role to suit the circumstances. He showed me how as he led us through a few more alleyways, across a small marketplace until we reached the band of gipsies or, as they are more popularly called, 'Minions of the Moon, — Children of the Night'. When we entered their encampment it was like entering another world: they paint their faces red or yellow and their bodies and heads are covered in fantastic costumes, embroidered turbans and brightly coloured scarves. They have little bells around their wrists and ankles so there is a melodious tinkle whenever they move. They did not prevent us approaching but stared woodenly, accepting us as the breeze that blows or the soil beneath their feet. Philippe took us to their leader, a tall, grizzled man with greasy locks falling down to his shoulder, a scar under his right eye and gold ear-rings glittering in his ear lobes. Villon talked to him in a foreign tongue and the fellow smiled, clasping Villon by the hand but continuing to look askance at me.

"Do you know who this is?" Villon asked, pointing at me.

The gipsy leader walked closer and stared.

"He is the Englishman, Ralph Croft," he replied in halting French. "He used to be called Scaramac. He was arrested, sentenced to death and put in the Bastille; later, the Duke of Orleans pardoned him. He now works on some secret mission which does not affect us, the common people, but might the throne of France.

He smiled in a dazzling show of white teeth, came closer and felt the quality of my cloak, enjoying the surprised look on my face. True, I was known in the Faubourg Saint-Antoine but how did these people know of me and what I was doing?

"They say," the gipsy leader continued, "that Monsieur Scaramac or Monsieur Croft may try to escape, not to the Channel ports because Croft is wanted dead or alive in England, but perhaps to Spain, north to Germany or east to the Rhineland."

I turned and stared at Villon.

"What is this?" I said.

"They say," the gipsy leader continued, "that the Regent has circulated his description to everyone." He looked up, his sinister blue eyes enjoying my discomfort. "If you escape, there is a bag of gold on your head dead or alive in France. However," the gipsy turned and smiled at Villon, "soldiers can be bribed but we cannot. We know you, Englishman, because the Templars have told us about you. They, too, have promised a great reward if you try to escape. My people know of you, not only here but elsewhere. If we find your corpse we can have your clothes and all you carry. If we capture you alive, we stand to gain more gold and silver than the Regent would ever offer." He shrugged. "Of course, Monsieur, you could flee, perhaps to Austria, to the darkness of Transylvania, but one day, in three, four or five months' time, my people would find you and, depending on their mood, kill you or take you prisoner."

He turned away and continued his canting talk with Villon.

Villon gave the man some gold, the fellow shrugged, looked hungrily once more at my cloak and sauntered off. Villon led me back through those narrow desolate streets to the carriage. I got in and slumped in the corner.

"Whatever I do," I said, "I am caught. If I stay, God knows what the Regent will do. If I flee, not only will every royal official in France be looking for me but those gipsies and Moon people as well."

Villon just sat opposite me and tapped the carriage roof for the driver to pull away.

"Monsieur," he replied eventually.

"At least I have warned you. If you escape you are a dead man. If you do escape, make sure you change your appearance like that Egyptian back there. Of course, you might elude the Regent but never the Templars."

"Who are they?" I asked.

Villon shrugged and, feeling under the seat, drew out a wine-skin and two cups. He handed one to me and filled both of them to the brim.

"I am a businessman, Englishman, not an historian. You want to buy English cloth without paying custom, I can do that. You want someone killed for a price, that can be arranged. You want a whore, she will be yours. A witch to make a love potion." He sipped greedily from the cup. "That poses no problems, but the Templars?" He shrugged. "What do I know of them? They say many years ago the Templars were a great fighting order, monks in armour who rode out against the infidel and showed no mercy. They grew rich, they had relics." He lowered his voice. "The true cross, the shroud which covered Christ, the veil Veronica used to wipe the good Saviour's face as he was led to Calvary. Oh, the Templars grew rich. They became bankers, international financiers. Their house in Paris held more treasure than Charlemagne's coffers ever did."

Villon drank once more from the cup and smacked his lips, relishing the full-blown taste of the wine. "The kings of France became jealous of them. They listened to stories about the Templars, how they worshipped a three-faced god, practised the black arts and raised demons. So the French king struck. In one night the great order of the Templars was destroyed. They were arrested, hanged, gibbeted and disembowelled. The French kings took their treasure and their houses. The Templars disappeared." He paused. "But not all of them. Some of them hid, swearing eternal vengeance against the crown of France, building up secret cells, not only in France, but England,

Italy, North Africa, using the wealth and knowledge they had managed to hide."

"Do you believe this?" I interrupted.

He shrugged.

"Sometimes, no. But then strange things happen and their presence is felt. Someone is found dead, a favour is asked or a wrong righted. Such things are done mysteriously by strangers who speak from the darkness, their only sign being the cross you drew."

"But you," I snapped. "You could help me escape?"

Villon nodded.

"Yes, I could, but one thing I have learnt about the Templars. They are not concerned about me or about the law. They plot continuously against the French crown. If you help them they never forget, if you harm, their interests they will strike back." He stopped and shook his head. "What kind of organisation," he whispered, "can use the Egyptians, the Moon people to carry out their business not

151

just in Paris but in the flat fields of Holland or the dark woods of Hungary? No one escapes them."

"If they are so powerful," I jibed, "why have they not toppled the kings?"

Villon leaned back in his seat, tapping his fingers on the side of the carriage.

"A good question that. I once asked it of the lawyer we helped." Villon edged closer. "Do you know his reply? The fellow gave me a short description of the fate of French kings in the last two hundred years."

He ticked the points off on his fingers, his eyes closed, screwed up in concentration.

"Charles VIII died banging his head against a cupboard in a darkened room. Henry II was killed at a tournament. All of Henry's sons died violent deaths. Henry IV was killed in his carriage whilst going through Paris. Louis XIII died mysteriously."

"The famous Sun King lived to a ripe old age," I replied.

"Yes, he did," Villon commented.

"But he faced plots, assassination attempts and had to attend the deathbed of both his son and grandson." Villon shrugged. "The present boy. Louis XIV's grandchild, may never reach manhood." He tapped me on the hand. "No Englishman, I cannot help you, but I tell you this. I know you are involved in uncovering the mystery of the Masked Man and that you ransacked his grave in St Paul's cemetery. I also suspect the Templars are involved in your great secret. They want to know the truth because it will help them."

"Could the Duke of Orleans be a Templar?" I asked.

Villon pursed his lips, his dark, handsome face now bereft of any humour.

"I have often wondered that," he said. "Monsieur Maurepas and Captain D'Estivet may simply be his tools, men he uses for his own purposes." He nodded his head. "Oh, yes, he could be. The younger brother of the King of France is always given the title Duke of Orleans and there has always been friction between them. Louis XIII hated his own brother whilst Gaston D'Orleans, the Sun King's brother, constantly posed as a homosexual because he knew his brother could not stand such men. There was little love lost between them."

He turned and smiled like a good-natured teacher playing with a pupil.

"It could well be, Monsieur, that you are correct. If so, the Duke of Orleans controls the Templars as he does the kingdom of France and he has you body and soul. No man can help you!"

I stared at this master criminal.

"You seem frightened of the Templars."

"Don't bait me, Englishman," Villon snapped back. "I know my power, where it begins and where it ends. Oh, I am interested in the Templars, I have studied them. Their Grand Master was executed on the 18th March 13 . . . " he closed his eyes, "yes, the 18th March

1314. He and three companions outside Notre Dame. They were strapped to stakes, brushwood piled high around them, then live coals were thrown in. The Templar Master burnt to death until all that was left was a smouldering, popping heap of coals." He turned and chewed at his lip. "I learnt this from an antequarian friend of mine. He has a shop in the Rue des Lacs. He said the Templars began their secret society the very night the Grand Master died. Some refugees of the Order swam the Seine, crawled across the mud to the execution ground and there in the darkness dug through the ashes and hot charcoal before swimming back across the river with the bitter, acrid bones of the last Grand Master clenched tightly in their mouths." He grinned. "What do you think of that, Englishman, eh? Would you do that? Would I? We, who believe in nothing but ourselves?"

"Your knowledge of the Templars is sharp," I said. "Are you one?"

Villon filled his wine cup then tapped

on the carriage top to tell the coachman to go faster.

"If I was, I wouldn't tell you!" He smiled. "You know, the Templars' castle still remains in Paris and every year at noon on the 18th March they place a great placard on the gate. God knows how it arrives there. It bears the great Templars cross and one word, 'Remember!'"

Villon pulled his cloak more firmly about him. I proffered my wine cup to be refilled and stared at the cushioned carriage top. Here was I, a Cornish lad, who had done nothing more than be born in unfortunate circumstances with a penchant for mischief and now I was involved in this. Villon was right, I have never cared for anything because I suppose no one has ever cared for me. The world is a market. You pass through and take what you want and spare not a second thought for what goes on around you. Religion? I thought of the fat vicar in Cornwall with his red face and mouth full of nothing.

Of the rich who allow the poor to starve at their gates. Sometimes in London I would question the Jacobites, young men quite prepared to die for something, yet that, too, was different, something tangible. But the Templars, secret groups committed to redressing centuries-old wrongs? Or was it just the human love of conspiracy, treason and betrayal? I remembered Abigail, my young wife of just a few weeks in London. Did she really love someone else? Or did she just love the intrigue and the bitter-sweet taste of betrayal? I glanced across at Villon as he slouched, eyes half closed. Somehow Villon believed that the cause of the Templars and the fate of the Man in the Iron Mask were linked. But why was he helping me?

"I am not asking you to trust me, the fellow drawled as if he could read my thoughts. "You were sent to find information. The Duke of Orleans may well be the Grand Master of the Templars. If I help him, he will help me. Anyway, I like you, Englishman, and the Duke of Orleans may just be an old woman, in which case he should have asked my permission before he plucked you from the Faubourg Saint-Antoine for his own uses."

"Do you think," I asked abruptly, "the Masked Man could have been a Templar?"

"It's possible," Villon replied after a while. "Our beloved Sun King, Louis XIV, faced many plots. Some of them carefully organised conspiracies, the most dangerous being in 1673 just after the anniversary of the death of the Grand Master of the Templars. An attempt was made to ambush the King's carriage as he travelled north to lead his armies in Holland."

"Tell me," I interrupted tactfully, "if Louis or his descendants were overthrown whom do the Templars see as the true royal line?"

"You should ask Monsieur Maurepas. He is the archivist. But, from what I can gather, the Templars look to the

158

House of Lorraine, who are direct descendants of the long-haired King, the Merovingians."

"And is there a claimant still alive?"

"Oh, yes," Villon replied, "somewhere. But the French kings always lock any notable ones up in a tower or desolate prison. Louis XIV did this to the aged Henri de Lorraine, Duc de Guise. The poor unfortunate died in prison on the Island of Ste Marguerite."

I sat up in astonishment. Villon had mentioned the same prison which had housed the Masked Man. The master criminal laughed.

"No, no, Englishman! Do not jump to conclusions. The Duc de Guise was in his 80's when he died and he was never brought to the Bastille."

I sat back. What a pity! Yet Villon was correct. Henri de Lorraine may have been feared by Louis but he was far too old to be the person we were looking for. My mind teemed with what I had learnt. I sat daydreaming and was jolted awake as the carriage clattered over cobbles and the driver began to swear and crack his whip. The noise outside the carriage grew as we had re-entered the Faubourg Saint-Antoine. Villon pulled the window covering aside and peered out.

"Stop!" he called to the coachman.

The carriage skittered to a halt. Villon got out, gesturing me to follow. I blinked and stared around, slightly dizzy at the noise and smells as I tried to make out where I was. Villon turned me gently by the shoulder and pointed up to the great looming mass of the Bastille.

"Englishman, we are finished. Monsieur Maurepas expects you." He put his hand on the carriage. "I wish you luck, Englishman. Be wary. Do not trust anyone, not even Monsieur Maurepas."

The master criminal climbed into his carriage seat.

"You must go, Englishman," he said softly. "I cannot help you any more."

He was about to tell the coachman to drive on but I grasped the door. Villon's eyes narrowed, his hand falling to the pistol he had undoubtedly hidden in the coach.

"Be careful, Englishman!"

"Monsieur Villon," I said. "I thank you for your help and assistance but you said Monsieur Maurepas had asked you for a second favour."

Villon looked away and smiled.

"Oh, quite simple," he replied. "Monsieur Maurepas said that if you tried to escape I was to kill you. Coachman, drive on!"

I stepped back and watched Villon's black and silver carriage rattle away over the cobbles, leaving me more desolate than I had ever felt in my life.

7

I DID not go back to the Louvre but straight to Maurepas' house; neither the archivist nor his assassin friend was there but Marie was. I remember the day being overcast, the house was dark and huge, wax candles burning in the entrance hall gave the place an eerie feeling, the half-light serving as a stage for the dancing shadows. Marie smiled as she opened the door and took me through to a small chamber off the hall. She had been poring over some accounts and she quickly closed the books, making those small, birdlike gestures with her hands.

"Did I want some chocolate? Some coffee?"

"No, brandy," I curtly replied.

The minx could read my lips and knew what I asking for but she grinned, shook her head and repeated the actions with her dainty fingers, insisting that I answer her the same way.

"Brandy!" I bellowed.

Again the smile. I sighed. She looked so beautiful and innocent that, coaxed by her eyes, I made the proper hand gestures for the drink I wanted. She gave me a small glass and, graciously ignoring my rudeness, sat me down to continue my education in that strange sign language. As I have said, I was an adept pupil and my anger and fury at Villon's parting words soon faded. I became fascinated by my beautiful teacher and her smooth, seductive ways. Without thinking I leaned across and kissed Marie gently on the lips. She did not turn away nor did she passionately respond. She let me kiss her gently again before stepping away and grinning mischievously at me.

I hoped such an amorous interlude would continue but Maurepas and D'Estivet brought it to an abrupt end. A terrible pounding on the door startled me (only then did I realise that, despite the archivist's apparent wealth, he kept no servants). Marie rose and, dabbing at her lips, she brushed by me and hurried to open the door. I heard angry voices as Maurepas and D'Estivet swept into the house, the archivist barking questions at Marie, not bothering to wait for answers. He entered the small counting-chamber, his face white with anger as he tried to curb his fury by biting hard on his lower lip. He stopped and glared down at me and my own anger swept back. Why should I care for this man? Why should I show courtesy to someone who had given orders for my death? D'Estivet stood behind him like some evil angel, a strange smile on his twisted face, his long, white fingers beating a silent tattoo on the hilt of his sword.

"Monsieur Maurepas," I retorted, "you are angry? Surely," I rose, drawing myself up to my full height, "I should be the one who is angry. You sent me into the Faubourg Saint-Antoine to search out criminals. I did so, achieving more success in one day than you or D'Estivet managed in weeks. I learnt a great deal. I thought you trusted me."

Now nothing amuses me more than myself pretending to be virtuous. I could feel my anger turn to sardonic humour at my own hypocrisy and I fought to keep my face impassive as my voice rose in righteous rage.

"You," I continued, jabbing a finger at Maurepas, "you gave orders for my murder if I should wander one inch from the path of righteousness! What trust is that?"

I glanced over his shoulder and saw Marie. (I am sure she was quietly laughing at me.) I stared into D'Estivet's cold, hard eyes.

"And you Captain?" I commented. "What are you going to do? Draw your sword? Well?"

I stepped past Maurepas to confront him.

"Why not, D'Estivet? Why not now?"

I watched that bastard's eyes. You know I could swear he was only an inch away from doing exactly what I asked and, if he had, I would have run like the legendary rabbit. D'Estivet, however, licked his lips and quickly glanced sideways as Marie, a worried frown on her face, caught him lightly by the arm. Maurepas sighed and tapped me gently on the shoulder.

"Come," he said. "Come, all of us into the hall. Marie, I smell brandy on our guest's breath, bring us all some. D'Estivet, for God's sake stop acting the duellist and relax."

Maurepas led us back into the hall. We sat in chairs around the small fire, its flames flickered feebly in the great hearth. Once Marie had served the brandy the archivist turned apologetically to me.

"Ralph," he began, "you have good cause to be angry but we, too, are frightened. If we allowed you to escape before this task was finished . . . "

His voice trailed off and I wondered

what really would happen when their task was done. I remained silent. I remembered de Renneville's words about the death of all those who had guarded the masked man, Giraut's grisly skeleton hanging in that apothecary's shop, Villon's face, sharp and cruel, and the crafty, clever eyes of Abbé Fleury. Marie silently filled my glass and smiled at me. D'Estivet sucked in his breath, hissing like a snake preparing to strike. Maurepas coughed. I suppose he expected some reply from me but I was learning to keep my mouth shut.

"Well, what did you learn in the Faubourg Saint-Antoine, Ralph?" he asked.

"I met the man called de Renneville," I replied. "You know him?"

Maurepas smiled sourly.

"I have heard of him."

"Well," I continued, "according to him the prisoner was closely guarded in the Bastille, his face was masked, he was kept under close custody all the time and . . . "

"And what else?" Maurepas asked quickly. "We know all that."

"The masked man was a prince."

The room fell quiet. I heard a clock chime out in the hallway and the faint sound of a cart clattering on the cobbles outside. Again I thought of Villon and Fleury and I wondered if the man who had been following me was still out there lurking in the shadows.

"You are sure about that?" D'Estivet quickly asked.

I repeated de Renneville's words and they heard me out.

"Hell's teeth!" Maurepas muttered. "But that does not match what we have learned." He put his hand inside his doublet and drew out a small roll of yellow parchment. "We have found the masked man's name." He looked at me and blinked, disappointment written all over his face. "His name," he continued wearily, "was Eustace D'Auger."

"You may remember," D'Estivet

interrupted, "how you went through the index of royal letters which gave us a summary of each document or warrant about the masked man. You found his name had been erased except for the first letter 'E'. Monsieur Maurepas," he continued smugly, "discovered the original letters. The names had been removed from there but then we found the drafts written in Louis XIV's own hand or that of his Minister of War. Here, the name is quite clear, it is Eustace D'Auger."

"Look," Maurepas continued, "this is the first letter dated the 19th July 1669. The Minister of War, Louvois, is writing to Saint-Mars to tell him to prepare a special cell for our prisoner whose arrest warrant has not yet been written. Go on, read it!"

I took the letter. (Maurepas later allowed me to transcribe it and other documents.) It read as follows:

"*Louvois to Monsieur Saint-Mars. Monsieur Saint-Mars, the King has commanded that I am to have a* man named Eustace D'Auger sent to Pignerol. It is of the utmost importance to His Majesty that D'Auger should be most securely guarded and that he must not be able to give anybody information about himself in any way, nor send letters to anyone at all. I am informing you of this in advance so that you can have a cell prepared in which you will put him securely, taking care that the windows of the place in which he is put do not give on to any places that can be approached by anyone and that there are multiple doors, for your sentries not to hear anything. You will yourself once a day, have to take enough food for the day to this wretch and you must on no account listen, for any reason whatsoever, to what he may want to say to you, always threatening to kill him if he ever opens his mouth to speak of anything but his necessities."

"Nine days later," Maurepas added, "Captain Vauroy in Dunkirk was sent the following order by the King himself to arrest D'Auger." He handed the second letter over.

"*Captain Vauroy, I am dissatisfied with the behaviour of the man named Eustace D'Auger and want to secure him. I am writing this letter to inform you that as soon as you shall see him, you are to seize him and to conduct him yourself in all safety to the citadel of Pignerol, where he is to be guarded by Captain Saint-Mars, to whom I am writing the attached letters so that the said prisoner shall be received and guarded there without difficulty. After which you are to return from there to render an account of that which you shall have done in execution of the present order.*"

"And finally," Maurpas commented, "this letter from the King to Saint-Mars himself. Here is the relevant extract."

"*I am sending to my citadel of Pignerol, in the charge of Captain Vauroy, Sergeant-Major of Dunkirk, the man named Eustace D'Auger. I am writing this letter to inform you that when the said Captain Vauroy arrives at my said citadel of Pignerol with the said prisoner, you are to receive him and hold him in good and safe custody, preventing him from communicating with anyone at all by word of mouth or by writing."*

I let all three manuscripts fall to the floor and gazed into the dying flames of the fire. I sensed my companions' disappointment. Eustace D'Auger, who was he? How could he be a prince? Why was he kept in prison for over thirty years? Why was he kept masked? Why had he not been brought to trial? I could feel my own disappointment, tinged with fear, welling within me. The Regent would not accept this. How could it be my passport to freedom? More likely to be dismissed as an admission of failure. And would I be sent back to the Bastille or even worse? Surely the name D'Auger was simply another veil of secrecy. I thought of the Italian spy, Matteoli, and turned excitedly to Maurepas.

"Look," I began, "de Renneville said the masked man was a prince. Maybe the name D'Auger was a fiction, a pseudonym to cover his true identity."

Maurepas shook his head and sighed, rubbing his face in his hands.

"We thought about that," he replied slowly. He looked up, his face lined and tired. "But remember, all that de Renneville repeated was gossip and, even so, he may still be correct. You see, Ralph, first there was a Eustace D'Auger. He came from a very noble family and he did disappear in or around 1669." He turned to D'Estivet. "Tell him," he said sourly, "tell him what you know."

D'Estivet slouched in his chair. I could see by his eyes that he, too, was disappointed though perhaps secretly pleased. I wondered if the bastard had read my thoughts and knew that if we failed I could not shrug it off.

"Come on, D'Estivet," I snarled. "I wait with bated breath. Tell me what you know!"

"Our dear Eustace," the soldier began, "was French, of noble birth, a Catholic and a soldier. He was born in 1639 and baptised here in Paris. His father was a Captain of the Musketeers and his mother a lady-in-waiting to Louis XIV's mother, Anne of Austria. Eustace fits many of the descriptions we have of the masked man; tall, well built, of noble birth, he could probably speak English, whatever good that did him." He shrugged.

"Go on!" I said sharply.

"That is all," he answered.

"That is all!" I got up, kicking my chair over. "But you haven't answered the question. Why was he imprisoned for thirty years? Why was he masked?"

D'Estivet took his sword hilt, pulling it across his lap as a reminder that he had power of life and death over me.

"Ah, Englishman," he said sardonically, "you may recollect that excellent memorandum you drew up for us. Remember, Louis XIV did not want the prisoner to communicate with anyone. Perhaps Eustace discovered some scandal. He was a swashbuckling rogue who lived in the shadow of the law. Perhaps he learnt something which our dead but glorious monarch wanted to be kept hidden."

"So, why not kill him?" I asked.

"Ah!" D'Estivet drew himself up in his chair. "But Louis XIV was scrupulous. It is not a crime to know something. Eustace came of good family. Someone like you, Croft, can have his throat cut, but not a D'Auger whose father was a captain in the musketeers and whose mother served the Queen."

I sat down. D'Estivet was right. A man like D'Auger fitted everything we knew about the masked man, even his age. According to the dates, D'Auger would be about thirty when he was arrested and in his mid sixties when he died. He might have learnt some scandal, and God knows there was enough at Louis XIV's court, and be given his life in return for his silence. Moreover, it would also solve the problem over his arrest at Dunkirk. A man like D'Auger would be well known, he would carry letters, warrants, and it would be very easy for the authorities there to arrest him. I felt like a drowning man clutching at straws.

"So, what did D'Auger know?" I asked wearily.

Maurepas rose, patting me affectionately on the shoulder as if I were some household pet.

"We don't know," he replied. "That's why you and D'Estivet are to go to the Rue des Bons Enfants to interview D'Auger's younger sister, Emile. She may tell us what her brother knew."

Within the hour D'Estivet and I had hired a carriage to take us to the Rue des Bons Enfants, a small thoroughfare in what used to be the fashionable part of Paris before the King moved his court to Versailles. Now it was quiet. The houses with their jutting stories seemed to have slept for centuries, the windows were shuttered, the gates leading to overgrown courtyards were firmly locked. A cat, skulking in a pile of refuse, stretched and snarled at us as we got down from the carriage outside a huge front door. Above us the house, five stories high, soared up to the sky.

"More a mausoleum," D'Estivet muttered as he grasped the rusting, iron bell-pull and brought it down with a crash which echoed along the hollow emptiness of the street like a death knell. No sound. I looked around. Far down the street a door opened and shut. I heard a man shout and the wail of a child. A dog barked and a light breeze rustled the rubbish which lay on either side of the street. D'Estivet took his tricorne hat off, his face now alive, a strange smile on his lips. His age-old eyes were sparkling at the prospect of danger. Again he grasped the iron bell-pull, tugging it until I thought he would waken the entire street. At last I heard the soft patter of footsteps and the rasp of rusty bolts being pulled back. Above us a bird, dark against the narrow strip of blue sky, flew from its nest under the eaves. The door swung open to reveal an old man, bent with age, his eyes rheumy in a tired, lined face, bloodless lips parted in a toothless smile.

"Madame D'Auger?" D'Estivet barked. "We wish to see Madame D'Auger!"

The old man cackled with laughter and shuffled his slippered feet.

"Visitors from the court, I presume?" he chuckled. "Always visitors from the court. Madame is so busy."

The fellow seemed as mad as a bat but he waved us forward into the dark, dusty passageway which smelt like a disused church, the stench of mould mingling with something more fragrant. We were led up a broad staircase, no light except for faint sunbeams lancing through the window at the top. The carpets were faded, the portraits hanging on the cracked walls dust-laden. We went down a long gallery, a lonely candle spluttered in its twisted, iron bracket: the old man stopped outside a door, knocked then opened it without waiting for an answer. The small room inside was as bare of comfort as it was of furnishings and reeked of old age and sickness. At the far side of the chamber, just underneath the broad windowsill sat a woman in a tall chair; her face under its mop of untidy white hair was thin and grey, her vein-knotted hands tightly gripped together. She stared at us, her eyes, round and pearly as pebbles.

"What is it, Bernard?" she called.

"Vistors from the court!" the servant grandly announced. "The King must want you back, Madame D'Auger. Perhaps our great days have returned. There will be candles in every socket, carpets on the floor, dancing in the hall below."

"Oh, Bernard," Madame D'Auger's voice was soft and cultured. "Bernard, get some wine for our visitors."

The old man stopped in full flow, pursed his lips, gave the deepest of bows and shuffled out. Madame

D'Auger indicated a bench and I moved it over.

"Bernard is quite mad," she commented as we introduced ourselves and sat down, her tired face creased in a smile as if relishing some secret thought. "But," she continued, "we are all mad, Messieurs, even you. What can you possibly want with an old lady?"

She waved one gloved hand, the white lace dirty and torn.

"An old lady," she murmured, "who has nothing but her memories."

"Just that," D'Estivet remarked bluntly. "We want your memories, Madame."

The old servant came padding back and placed a tall-stemmed Venetian glass in front of each of us. There was wine in none of them. Madame D'Auger just twitched in mild exasperation.

"Go away, Bernard," she said. "Our guests will enjoy the glass, I suppose they can imagine the wine."

The old man shuffled softly out.

180

"You talk of memories, Monsieur." Madame D'Auger glared at D'Estivet. Her small, dark eyes reflected an instant dislike for him.

"Madame," I tactfully intervened, "we are strangers, visitors in your house but we are here at the express command of the Regent."

The pinched face became more set.

"What does he want?" she said.

"Nothing," I murmured, "but he would like you to tell us about your brother Eustace."

The old lady leaned back in her chair and smiled.

"Our house," she murmured, "is one of the oldest in France. Our ancestor Ogier the Dane was one of the twelve lords of Charlemagne. He was with Roland at Roncesvalles. My grandfather, Adrian, was called 'The Man With the Iron Arm' because of his skill with the sword."

D'Estivet stiffened beside me. Strange, I reflected, how Eustace's grandfather had the adjective 'Iron' applied to him.

I also remembered that in card games, Hogier was the knave of spades, a card the French called the 'Valet'. My heart sank. Perhaps Maurepas was right. We had found the man and he would turn out to be nothing of consquence.

"My father, François," the old lady continued, her face now alive as memories took her back down the dusty years, "my father was also a great swordsman. In 1631 he became Captain of Cardinal Richelieu's Musketeers."

She paused and picked up the Venetian glass, clasping it in her old hands as if it were a talisman.

"You know," she murmured, "my father fought with D'Artagnan on the young Gascon's first day of service in the royal musketeers." She smiled at us. "You know the story? There was great rivalry between the Cardinal's musketeers and King Louis XIII's. D'Artagnan was helped by three others, Athos, Porthos and Aramis."

The old lady waved her hand. I looked around and glimpsed the small table with a half-filled wine decanter on it. I got up and filled our three glasses, all the time thinking about what the old lady had said. Another link with our mystery! D'Artagnan had arrested Fouquet and hadn't the famous swordsman recommended Saint-Mars to be the masked man's gaoler? I sat down and toasted the old lady with my glass. She sipped carefully from hers, before continuing.

"My parents had eleven children. All the boys, including Eustace, became soldiers. After my father's death, my mother continued to be lady-in-waiting to Queen Anne of Austria."

"And Eustace? What about Eustace?" D'Estivet interrupted testily.

"Eustace," Madame D'Auger continued smoothly, "was the black sheep of the family. You know, on one occasion he challenged his friend, Lauzun, to a duel in the presence of the King. During the fight Eustace's wig fell to the ground." The old lady stopped and giggled like some young girl. "The young King, Louis XIV, hated such violence but he spared Eustace, his mother and ours were great friends."

As Madame D'Auger sipped from her glass I looked at D'Estivet who just sat, chewing his lip; he shook his head despondently. I am sure we shared the same thoughts: if Eustace had dared to draw his sword, let alone fight in the royal presence, King Louis must have had a special affection for him. All seemed to fit. So, was this old lady the sister of the masked man? A self-confessed rogue whom Louis XIV loved and could not kill so, instead, he had sentenced him to a life of comfortable imprisonment? But why the secrecy?

I leaned forward.

"Madame," I asked, "this duel, was it the reason your brother fell from royal favour?"

The old lady tossed her head and cackled with laughter.

"Of course not! Let me see." She took another sip of wine and licked her lips. "It was April, no it was Easter 1659. Eustace and some friends went into the country to attend a party at a chateau. You know how it is?" She shook her head. "His companions were not, how shall we say, savoury. The trouble started on Good Friday morning, a day of fasting and abstinence. Eustace and his friends, however, ignored all of this. They started a debauch which lasted all day and most of the Easter weekend. They insisted on eating pork, saying it had been resurrected as a fish. Moreover, they seized one of the King's chaplains who had stopped off on his way to Paris and made him drunk as well as forcing him to witness their orgies." She stopped, embarrassed. "Eustace's friends were homosexual and, at that party, they made little attempt to hide it. Anyway," she concluded, "they were all punished."

"And Eustace fell from grace?" I asked.

"No! No!" she muttered. "There was

worse to come. Six years later Eustace was at Saint Germain where he got into an argument with a page and ran him through with his sword." The old lady sighed. "Eustace had to resign his commission. He stayed for a while with my brother Louis in the Rue de la Sourdière. After that, she shrugged, "he just disappeared."

D'Estivet stirred in his chair.

"But Madame, there must be more than that, surely?"

I saw a faint smile flicker across the old woman's face. D'Estivet was right but she had taken such a dislike to my companion I doubted whether he would ever get the truth out of her. I looked around that deserted chamber, the peeling walls, the faded carpets covered with flakes of plaster which had fallen from the ceiling. It had grown dark, the shadows were closing in. Perhaps I am too imaginative but I sensed a presence there. Perhaps it was the old lady herself. She was concealing something.

"Your brothers, Madame?" I asked.

"All dead," she replied softly.

"Madame," I insisted, "there must be more. Surely? What did your brother Eustace do? Why did he disappear? Where? For God's sake, Madame?"

The old lady rocked in her chair. I looked sideways at D'Estivet. His hand had fallen to the hilt of his beloved sword. I remembered his boast that once he had drawn it he would kill, that he even slept with it. The only time, or so he proudly declared, he ever took it off was when he was frolicking with his other 'sword' in the combat of love. I looked at his thin lips and narrow eyes. He would kill this old woman. I saw her eyes widen with alarm. She was old and shrewd enough to recognise the danger. I took her thin, cold hand in mine and raised it to my lips, kissing the veined fingers gently. She squeezed my hand in return as if acknowledging some secret bond of friendship.

"Madame," I insisted, "please tell us."

"You could," she murmured, "ask the Marquise de Brinvilliers or La Reynie." Her voice rose. "Or, better still, Madame La Voisin!"

D'Estivet squirmed in his seat and Madame D'Auger cackled with laughter. She leaned forward.

"Monsieur Croft. I have said enough. Your companion knows what I am talking about. Now," she picked up a small bell from beneath her chair and rang it, "now, you must go!"

D'Estivet needed no second bidding. Indeed, I was surprised by his apprehension and, when the old retainer Bernard showed us down the stairs, D'Estivet left as quietly as a child. Outside it was growing dark, the streets were silent and deserted except for the mournful baying of some dog. D'Estivet wrapped his cloak around him and walked as if I no longer existed.

"Captain," I said, "I do not like you and you do not like me. Yet you are a born soldier. Perhaps one of France's greatest swordsmen."

D'Estivet stopped and turned towards me. He nodded imperceptibly, acknowledging the compliments.

"So, Englishman, what do you want to say?"

I pointed back to the old house.

"When Madame D'Auger mentioned those names, I sensed your fear, your alarm. What is the matter?"

D'Estivet came so close I could smell the faint odour of corruption from his rotting teeth.

"Englishman," he said quietly, "you have not heard of the Affair of the poisons?" He looked around at the shuttered houses and shivered. "I am frightened of nothing living, nor dead, but those who dabble in black magic, who can call up demons," he nodded, "I fear them. Those who engage in secret poisons, men and women, who offer you a cup of wine in friendship and watch you die in agony. Oh, yes, I fear them."

"And the names that Madame D'Auger mentioned, they were all poisoners?"

D'Estivet turned and spat.

"All of them. Followers of the devil except La Reynie. He was the Inspector of Police in Paris who tracked them down. The scandal reached even the crown. Most of the papers were burnt by Louis XIV himself shortly before he died. If our masked man was involved in these crimes then it is a perilous path we tread. But, come, Monsieur Maurepas will be waiting for us."

We walked further up the street. My thoughts were miles away when three figures suddenly appeared to block our path. I was daydreaming so much I would probably have tried to push by them but D'Estivet gripped me by the arm and my heart lurched as I looked again. All three were masked; their faces under the broad-brimmed, plumed hats, were hidden by the sort of vizards ladies wear when they go to the opera or theatre with their lovers. Yet there was nothing pleasant or debonair about those three: their cloaks had been pushed back over their shoulders, their swords and daggers hung menacingly from broad, leather belts. Killers, assassins.

My alarm increased. I had no sword, dagger or pistol to protect myself and I panicked. Perhaps they were here only to kill me. Perhaps D'Estivet would just step aside but, at the time, the Captain seemed to be made of sterner stuff. He merely stopped, smiled and looked all three up and down.

"Messieurs," he said softly. "You are in our way. Step aside!" His hands fell beneath his cloak. "Messieurs," he repeated. "You can see my companion is unarmed. We wish no trouble."

The three bullies stood there silently. D'Estivet gripped my arm, we stepped back a few paces and my fear increased.

"Messieurs," D'Estivet said with a ghastly smile on his face, "I beg you to step aside."

He got his reply as our three

adversaries drew their swords and daggers. The middle one stepped forward.

"Monsieur, it is good to hear an officer beg." The accent was guttural, foreign. "Perhaps once more and we will let you pass."

"D'Estivet," I hissed, noting how a muscle high in the Captain's cheek was beginning to tremble. "D'Estivet, there are three of them!"

"What did your companion say?" our assailant asked. "Is he insulting us?"

"Oh, no," D'Estivet replied. "He said there are three of you but he is wrong."

"What do you mean?"

"I mean," D'Estivet replied, "there are not three but two!"

Drawing his hands from beneath his cloak, he cocked the small pistol he carried and shot the fellow straight through the heart. The other two rogues watched their leader crumple to the ground and, with a cry of rage, they rushed for D'Estivet. He flung the pistol at them, swept back his cloak and, drawing sword and dagger, engaged both of them with the consummate skill of a fencing master. He kept both opponents together, using his weapons to parry their blows, turning them away from me whilst protecting his own back against the wall of a house. The two attackers, perhaps not the most intelligent of men, allowed D'Estivet to determine the fight, not realising how easy it would have been for one of them to step sideways and deal with me. I jumped up and down, shouting for help, attempting to look busy and finally managed to secure the dead assassin's sword. D'Estivet, however, turned and grimaced at me, his face had become boyish, losing its long, hungry look.

"You see, Englishman," he called out. "How I am one of France's greatest swordsmen!"

He stopped speaking as both assailants closed with him again in a clash of steel and muttered oaths but D'Estivet was brilliant, his sword was a circling wheel of steel which protected him. His coolness, mocking laughter and shouted observations only made the attackers more impetuous. One of them, stung to fury must have remembered me and turned to where I stood. D'Estivet, however, moved with him. Using the dagger to fend off one assailant, he turned and gently drove his sword straight into the man's neck and the fellow collapsed, choking on his own blood. D'Estivet now advanced, driving the last attacker back. The man broke off, panting for breath, and screamed something at D'Estivet. I did not understand it. I think it was German. D'Estivet just laughed.

"Now Englishman," he called over his shoulder. "I shall kill this fellow on the count of five. One," D'Estivet moved forward, "two, three!" his sword clashed with the assassin's. "Four!" I saw the assassin's sword arm thrust back, "and five!" D'Estivet suddenly lunged on one knee, driving his sword straight into the opponent's belly. The fellow died as he fell. D'Estivet wiped his sword and dagger on the man's cloak, "Good exercise, Englishman! he called out. "I enjoyed that."

I just stared open-mouthed at him. He squeezed my cheek with his fingers.

"I thank you, Monsieur, for not interfering. Now, let us see if we know them."

8

WE turned the corpses over, now nothing more than bundles of soggy rags lying in the mud. D'Estivet removed the mask from each, scrutinising them carefully. One was young, dirty blond hair fringed a face as fresh and clean as a farm boy's, his eyes were closed as if he had just fallen asleep. The other two were older, their hair and whiskers iron grey, their blood-shot eyes stared blankly up at the overcast sky.

"I don't recognise any of them," D'Estivet muttered.

I joined him, ignoring his angry look as I slipped the cheap rings from their fingers and the slender purses off their belts.

"You never know," I said, glaring back at him, "when you may need extra money."

I looked at the strange coins.

"They were Germans," I said. "Probably former mercenaries."

D'Estivet just shrugged, giving me that deprecating look as if he were superior to considering his victims or their belongings. A small crowd had begun to collect, doors quietly opening, women stood on the thresholds staring blankly at us, while behind them young children slipped out, eager to see what their parents were so interested in. Others, too, were beginning to join us, those shadowy denizens of the slums and alleyways. The human scavengers who could smell blood and sniff out easy pickings. They would have come closer but D'Estivet called a young boy over, twirling a coin at him which the child caught as deftly as a trained dog would a bone.

"Go on, lad!" D'Estivet called out. "Tell the provost what you have seen. Say that Captain D'Estivet sent you."

He made the boy haltingly repeat his words until the scruffy messenger had it word perfect, before sending him off, scurrying like a hare along the side of the buildings. D'Estivet ensured his hands were clean, adjusted his cloak and imperiously beckoned me on.

We walked out of that fearsome street and on to the boulevard back to the Louvre Palace. We strolled like two dignified gentleman taking the air. At last D'Estivet broke the silence, stopping and looking at me as if I had the answer.

"Who do you think sent those assassins?" he asked.

I shrugged.

"I don't know," I replied.

D'Estivet smirked.

"No, you wouldn't," he murmured, "nor would anyone who knew of my swordsmanship. Do you know," he continued, "I believe they were not sent to kill us."

"For what then?"

"I don't know. Perhaps threaten us, frighten us but something went wrong."

He shook his head and we walked

through the great gates of the palace, each of us lost in his own thoughts. The more I reflected, the more I considered D'Estivet was right. Our three attackers could have struck more silently, more quickly. I had the impression that they had been told to deliver a message but, taunted by D'Estivet, as well as their own bravado, they could not resist drawing their swords. I knew little about court life but I considered D'Estivet's reputation as a swordsman was both feared and well known. A thought chilled my heart and sent my blood racing. Had they come for D'Estivet or was it me they were after, hoping that D'Estivet's dislike of me would make him a silent but co-operative bystander? The thought made sense. The one thing the assassins had not reckoned with was D'Estivet's insufferable arrogance and his lust for killing.

We went back to our chamber in the Louvre. Maurepas was waiting for us. He took one look at D'Estivet's blood-and mud-spattered cloak.

"Gentleman!" he cried. "What on earth has happened?"

Maurepas grasped D'Estivet by the shoulders and threw a glance at me. In abrupt tones D'Estivet described our visit to Madame D'Auger and our meeting with the three assassins. Maurepas heard him out, nodding carefully, interjecting the odd question, a look of deep concern in his eyes. God forgive me, I sensed there was something wrong. Perhaps it was just my evil heart and suspicious mind but Maurepas seemed to care too much. He was a little too solicitous and I wondered if the archivist's friendship for D'Estivet was outweighed by other considerations. Maurepas questioned me but I repeated faithfully what D'Estivet had said.

"Who could it be?" Maurepas asked.

I just shook my head. I had kept quiet about the visit of the Abbé Fleury, about my suspicions of being followed or Villon's revelations about the secret order of the Templars. At all times my one and only maxim is that discretion is the better part of valour.

Maurepas summoned a servant who brought a jug of water and a bowl and napkin for D'Estivet to wash his hands and face. After he had finished his toilette D'Estivet asked me to leave and remain outside in the corridor. He looked knowingly at Maurepas and said he had learnt things from Madame D'Auger which, for the time being, had to be kept secret. Maurepas agreed.

"Don't worry, Ralph," he said, showing me out. "I will see what this is about. But remember what the Regent said. We are delving into secret and dangerous matters. You must only know what you need to know."

I was pushed gently through the door. A Swiss guard appeared as if from nowhere and briskly ushered me further along the gallery to ensure I did not eavesdrop. I grinned to myself. Maurepas had the full measure of me. Of course, given half the opportunity,

I would have listened.

I stood there for hours; beyond the thick glass windows the day died and darkness fell. I listened to the noise of the palace as it came to life for its endless round of card games, fetes, masques and dances. Officials, arrogant in their own importance, brushed superciliously by me, followed by a gaggle of courtiers, their silk clothes drenched in perfume, their hair pomaded a silver white. They looked me up and down and hurried by giggling, holding their scented pomanders to their noses as if I were some animal who had wandered in from the alleyways; I thought of the three assassins, probably now stripped, stiffening, cold in some smelly, rat-infested mortuary. What did those men want? I almost wished D'Estivet had not been so quick with his sword. I thought about Madame D'Auger, the old lady with the knowing eyes and secretive ways.

At last, totally bored, I examined

the great portraits hanging on the wall. Most were of King Louis XIV, the Sun King, in many of his different poses; emperor, personification of the deity, courtier, and brilliant general. I studied the proud face, the arrogant eyes, high cheekbones and fleshy nose. A memory stirred. Something I had seen in Madame D'Auger's house struck a chord in my mind but I could not recall it. Down the gallery the door opened. Maurepas came bustling out, smiling apologetically at me. Half an hour later he returned, carrying a small casket, the same one he had used the first morning I had met him. He held it as if it contained something precious and disappeared back into the room again. It must have been late evening. A clock chimed, eight or nine o'clock, and I heard the faint strains of music from one of the banqueting halls below. Maurepas opened the door and waved me back into the room. He smiled ingratiatingly as he gestured me towards a seat and served me with a brimming cup of white wine and a dish of wafer-thin sweetmeats. I liked that about Maurepas; he might have been a murderous bastard but he had more manners than D'Estivet who sat lounging at the table as if he hadn't a care in the world. The lunatic had probably forgotten that only hours earlier he'd sent three men to meet their Maker. The table in front of him was littered with papers and the casket Maurepas had brought was empty. The archivist took his seat at the head of the table, clawing the manuscripts back into an orderly pile as if we were all part of some well-meaning card game.

"Thank you for waiting, Ralph," he began. "But you can appreciate that Madame D'Auger referred to matters which are highly secretive. Affairs of state which can only be known by a few." He smiled falsely. "I had to see no less a person than the Regent who has heard good reports of us and of you," he added patronisingly. "He has given permission for you to know secrets which, if divulged, would send any other man to the scaffold."

"Oh, for God's sake!" D'Estivet interrupted. "Who can Croft tell?" He smiled icily at me. "I always look after you, don't I, Ralph?"

I blew my nose, it was about the only rude response I could safely make. Maurepas cleared his throat and leaned across.

"Ralph," he murmured, "you heard Madame D'Auger mention the name Brinvilliers and the 'Affair of Poisons'. Do you know anything about it?"

I shook my head.

"Well," he began, "in 1668, the year before our masked man was arrested, the Marquise de Brinvilliers, a sweet old lady, was nursing her father through a terrible illness. She visited him often in hospital and extended her ministrations to other unfortunates there." Maurepas licked his lips. "To cut a very cruel as well as a long story short, the Marquise's father died, then her two brothers and, finally, her husband.

Naturally, people became suspicious and, through a government informant, it was discovered that de Brinvilliers was the devil incarnate, probably one of the greatest poisoners in the history of that evil art. She had poisoned her own family and anyone else she visited on her so-called missions of mercy, in order to experiment with certain chemicals. Most of those she tended in hospital died horrific deaths."

Maurepas nodded at D'Estivet to continue as he rose to fill our wine cups.

"De Brinvilliers," D'Estivet began, "managed to escape and went into hiding but the scandals she caused began ripples of alarm. The government heard stories about a vast network of poisoners in Paris, who not only carried out their malicious, evil practices but also indulged in black magic and demon-worshipping. In 1670 Henrietta, sister-in-law to Louis XIV, died in agony. At the same time, priests from Notre Dame informed the King in an anonymous memorandum how many ladies of the court were confessing to murder by poison."

"How is this connected with the Man in the Iron Mask?" I asked.

"Ah!" Maurepas sat down, waving his finger at me as if he were a schoolmaster. "In 1676 Louis had appointed La Reynie as Chief of Police here in Paris. Now La Reynie searched out and arrested de Brinvilliers. She was tried, beheaded, and her body burnt at the stake. But she, too, intimated that others were involved. La Reynie achieved success when two of her accomplices turned King's Evidence. They confessed to everything and revealed a network of poison and black magic which led even up to the throne. Louis XIV's mistress, Madame de Montespan, by whom the King had a number of illegitimate children, was named. Torture was used, bribes given and La Reynie established — that Madame de Montespan had used love potions on the King and involved herself in black masses where infants were sacrificed, devils raised and spells cast to keep the King, our beloved Louis XIV, under de Montespan's influence."

I gingerly touched the pile of manuscripts.

"And these tell you that?" I asked.

"No." Maurepas leaned back in his chair like some smug village priest. "Louis set up a special court called the 'Chambre Ardente' to try all the people implicated but the revelations were so shocking that the King eventually closed it down and drew a great veil of secrecy over the affair. Just before he died, Louis XIV himself burnt the records of his court, but what he didn't know was that La Reynie had kept his own files." Maurepas tapped the manuscripts gently. "These belonged to La Reynie. Now," Maurepas continued, "our man, D'Auger. During de Brinvilliers' trial, La Reynie seized a magician named Belot. He was brought before the Chambre, tied to an apparatus which crushed his knees under planks as they were hammered down by mallets. During this interrogation Belot went back to the beginning of the affair of poisoning and named the man who had supplied the ring of poisoners with their potions and concoctions. This drug-seller had been active about 1667."

"And his name was D'Auger?" I added.

"Exactly," Maurepas replied. "Belot described him as tall, young and well built and living in or near the Rue de la Sordière, where Eustace D'Auger's brother, Louis, lived."

I looked down at the yellowing pile of manuscripts. Everthing we knew indicated that D'Auger was our masked man. He was of noble birth; he had powerful connections at the French court. He could probably speak English and was within the age range of the man we were seeking. He could very well be the prisoner for he had been involved, years earlier, in that blasphemous Easter week-end.

I squirmed on the chair. Everything made sense. A powerful family like the D'Augers, Eustace being the black sheep, disgracing his military uniform, becoming involved in the seamy Paris underworld and eventually arrested and incarcerated for life, but there had to be more.

"What's wrong?" D'Estivet casually asked. "You look puzzled, Englishman."

I rose and walked around the room.

"There's a piece missing to this puzzle," I said. "I can understand Louis XIV sparing Eustace D'Auger because of his family connections, but why the tremendous secrecy? Everybody knew who D'Auger was. Why the mask? Why the veil of silence?"

"Perhaps D'Auger knew something about the Affair of Poisons," D'Estivet commented.

I looked at my two companions. Both were watching me curiously. I could sense their disappointment. They, too, wanted the identity of the masked man to be more than that of a common criminal.

"I know what you are saying, Ralph," Maurepas commented, the excitement in his voice barely concealed. "Why didn't Louis just kill Eustace? There is something else, isn't there?"

I looked at the portrait of Louis XIV which dominated the library. My mind went back to that ancient, dusty house in the Rue des Bons Enfants and I burst into peals of laughter.

"I know it!" I cried excitedly, like some young boy who has discovered a present hidden by his parents. "I think I know it!"

Both Maurepas and D'Estivet got up. Their faces were grave, no humour, no excitement there.

"Tell us, Ralph," Maurepas said softly. "What do you know?"

I saw D'Estivet's hand fall to the hilt of that terrible sword but I did not care. I felt like a man who had been lost in a dark wood and had suddenly stumbled on to the path out.

"I shall tell you in the morning," I replied firmly, thoroughly enjoying my new-found power.

D'Estivet tapped his fingers on the scabbard of his sword.

"Tell us now, Croft."

I walked up to him and stared into those soulless eyes.

"Don't bully me, D'Estivet!" I snarled. "What are you going to do? Kill me? What would the Regent say to that, eh?"

I saw the assassin's face relax a little.

"Captain D'Estivet," Maurepas interrupted quietly, "I think Master Croft is going to tell us, but he has a price."

I smiled sweetly at the archivist.

"Monsieur Maurepas, you are a man of great sensivity. I wish a full pardon to be given to me by the Regent, now. I want a hundred pounds of silver." I stared at D'Estivet. "I want a sword, a dagger and a pistol. I also, for the first time since I came to this benighted place, want a decent meal, a bottle of the best claret as well as the company of the costliest and most professional courtesan. If these requests are granted to me before eight o'clock tomorrow. I shall tell you why Eustace D'Auger became the Man in the Iron Mask!"

That night I ate a meal I would dream of in the Elysian Fields. It was served by the prettiest whore the court could find though that wouldn't have been difficult, there were many in the palace under different titles and names, the Marquise this, the Marquise that. The young lady who came tripping up the great staircase and stepped quickly into my room was one of these blue-bloods, the Marquise de Montforêt or something or other. Nevertheless, she served me well, her skin shimmering; lustrous, reddish hair falling down to alabaster shoulders. We passed a memorable night. Early in the morning when I woke for a while, she was gone, nothing remained but the fragant smell of her perfume. I thought about Marie and felt guilty.

I wondered if D'Estivet had told her about the courtesan and concluded that the bastard probably had.

I fell back asleep, dreaming of Marie, and was given a rude awakening by Maurepas pounding on the door. When I opened it he stood there looking like some local vicar coming round to catch the sinner. D'Estivet just leaned smirking against the doorpost.

"You enjoyed yourself, Monsieur?" he asked mockingly.

I ignored him and looked at Maurepas.

"You kept the rest of the bargain?" I asked.

Maurepas slid his hand beneath his doublet and drew out a small, white roll of parchment which he handed to me. I undid the green silk and studied the contents carefully. It was a pardon issued under the Regent's name and seal:

"To Ralph Croft, alias Scaramac, for all offences committed in the kingdom of France since the time of entry to this day, etc. etc.

I licked my lips and looked at the document carefully. It gave the bastards a way out. If I committed any serious crime after today, they could probably arrest me. I shrugged. It would do well enough. And the money? Two clinking, leather bags were handed over.

"The weapons?" I queried.

Maurepas smiled and nodded. He clicked his fingers and a Swiss guard appeared, holding a broad, black leather belt. It held a sword, a dagger, a wicked-looking horse pistol and an ammunition pouch. I grabbed these and stashed them under the bed. Maurepas watched me.

"You drive a hard bargain, Ralph," he commented. "But come, you would have got all this as a reward for your services anyway. So, enough of these games. What do you know?"

I took great pleasure telling them to wait outside while I carried out my toilette and dressed quickly. Then I took them back to the long library in which we always worked.

"You will need," I said as we came beneath the picture of Louis XIV, "a squad of soldiers and a cart. They are to go the house of Madame D'Auger in the Rue des Bons Enfants and take down all the paintings which are hanging on the walls there."

"This is nonsense!" D'Estivet snapped. "Why do we need paintings from that old bitch's house? How can they help us?"

Maurepas glanced shrewdly at me.

"You know something, don't you?" he murmured softly.

"I suspect something," I added quietly. "I can't prove it, but at least I can persuade you that I am not talking nonsense."

D'Estivet argued for a while. Maurepas heard him out but then shook his head.

"I want to investigate this," he said. "It is worth following even if it leads to a stone wall. I agree with Ralph. We may have unmasked the mysterious prisoner. We know he was a rogue but still we haven't answered the question why Eustace wasn't simply executed. Why was he treated with such reverence? Masked and hidden away? That we have to establish."

After more grumbling from D'Estivet, Maurepas and I had our way. Servants were summoned, a scrivener was called in, bringing his tray of pens, quills and parchment. Maurepas wrote a few notes and handed them over to D'Estivet who, glowering at me, stalked out of the room. Maurepas left me, saying I should stay and he would have food and wine sent up. I was not to leave the library. I agreed, there was nothing else to do. I thought of the young lady who had entertained me the previous evening and I wondered if I could search her out. I opened the door but Maurepas had stationed two Swiss guards there. They were friendly enough, standing to attention when I appeared, but their intent was obvious. They were there to protect me, so one of them said in his harsh guttural voice. I knew different. They were there to guard me and make sure I did not slip away.

Late in the afternoon D'Estivet returned. He came marching up the staircase like an emperor, his head held as arrogantly as a peacock; behind him, swearing and cursing, came a trail of soldiers, each carrying a portrait. The servants bustled in with thick, felt cloths and began to dust the paintings. I think Maurepas, who examined one carefully, knew what I was going to say. He tried hard to control his excitement but I could see his chest heave and two red spots appear high in his cheeks. When the room was cleared, I looked at the paintings and saw the one which had caught my eye as we went down that dusty staircase at the D'Auger house. I picked it up, pulled across a small ladder used in the library to reach books high on the shelves, climbed it and held the portrait against that of King Louis XIV.

"Look!" I cried triumphantly, like a child revealing a mystery. "Look at it for God's sake, gentlemen!"

"They are twins," Maurepas whispered. "The story is correct then. The masked man was a twin brother of Louis XIV!"

"Nonsense!" I cried. "Look, down in the left corner of the painting, see the artist's name and that of his sitter, Eustace D'Auger, the date 1666."

I clattered down the ladder as Maurepas and D'Estivet came over. The archivist looked subdued, lost in his own thoughts, working out the implications of what I had said. D'Estivet had lost some of his cynicism. He just stood there, a strange smile on his face.

"This is Eustace D'Auger," I said, tapping the painting. "That is Louis XIV. Look, the same broad face, the high, narrow eyes, the cheekbones, even the spoilt twist to the mouth. I mean no offence," I added hastily, "but these men come from the same womb."

"How could that be?" Maurepas whispered.

"Well," I said, "let's go back to the original story. You remember, Monsieur?" I turned to Maurepas. "You said that Louis XIII," I pointed at the painting, "this king's father, hated women, hated Spaniards and hated his wife. But there is one thing you did not tell me. Something I know from common gossip and scandal. If he hated his wife, he hated his brother even more. Gaston, the Duke of Orleans, ancestor of the present Regent. Now, as his reign progressed," I continued in a hurry, "Louis XIII realised that unless his wife, Anne of Austria, bore a child, the crown would go to his hated brother."

"Go on!" Maurepas murmured.

"You also alleged, quoting a doctor, I forget the actual details, about Louis XIII's inability to beget an heir, about maturing sexually rather late. Can you remember it?"

Maurepas took the painting out of my hands, laid it on the table and stood over it.

"Yes, I remember that," he murmured. "Let me see."

I felt D'Estivet come up behind me. He was tense, I could sense his excitement, as if he was willing me on to the conclusion of my argument. Maurepas also glanced at him and I caught a look of rancour and dislike. Once again I wondered why, when each thought the other wasn't aware or looking, I caught this sense of rivalry between them.

"Monsieur Maurepas," I said, breaking into the archivist's reverie, "I was asking you about the doctor."

The archivist sat down and rubbed his face in his hands.

"There are many stories about Anne of Austria," he murmured. "Even now it is considered an offence to repeat some of the scurrilous stories published in a book twenty-five years ago. "Now, what was the title?"

"*The loves of Queen Anne*," D'Estivet interjected.

"Ah, yes. According to this, Louis XIV's mother had a love affair with the English Duke of Buckingham." The archivist shrugged. "Now most of this can be dismissed as scandal mongering. A more serious matter was Doctor Gondinet, he was physician to Queen Anne and attended an autopsy on her husband, Louis XIII. The findings of this autopsy were to be kept secret but Gondinet told his nephew, who published them in a pamphlet which asserted that Louis XIII had the testicles of a child and was incapable of begetting any children."

I pointed to the portrait.

"But this could be the mystery of Eustace D'Auger." I stood up. "Can't you see, I cried excitedly, "D'Auger's mother was a lady-in-waiting to Queen Anne! Her husband, François, was a consummate courtier as well as a prolific begetter of children." I paused for effect. "Did Francois D'Auger's father have an affair with Anne of Austria? Is he the real father of Louis XIV, hence the striking family resemblance?"

"And what about Louis XIV's brother?" D'Estivet queried.

I shrugged.

"With all due respect, who cares about the Duke of Orleans? The crown of France has descended through Louis XIV."

D'Estivet smiled wryly.

"It's possible," he murmured. "Perhaps Queen Anne's husband may have even connived at it. There is a close family resemblance. However," he waved his hand airily, "go out through the galleries of this palace, look at the portraits hanging there. You will find many men who look like the king because they aped his fashions, his looks, his mode of dress." D'Estivet snorted with laughter. "I have even seen a portrait of Saint-Mars, the masked man's gaoler; of Louvois, the

Minister of War, they all bear a close resemblance to Louis XIV." He tapped his hand on his sword hilt. "There is an added problem: courtiers not only aped royal fashions and modes, but the portrait-painters gave their work a twist so that the person sitting for them took on an aura of royalty." He glanced at the archivist. "Is that not so, Monsieur Maurepas?"

Maurepas shook himself out of his reverie.

"It's true," he murmured. "But there may be something in what Croft says." He wagged a finger at D'Estivet. "Louis XIV was born in 1638 but when he was conceived a year earlier his mother, Anne, was in disgrace and under house arrest here at the Louvre Palace. She was under the direct care of her husband's Chief Minister, Cardinal Richelieu."

"And Richelieu's Captain of Musketeers," I said, "was no less a person than the dashing François D'Auger, father of Eustace and perhaps the father of our great Sun King."

I wished I hadn't said that. Maurepas' eyes came up quickly, locking on to mine. I saw something there during those few seconds which made me shiver and feel frightened. I glanced away and looked at D'Estivet but he had the same close face and hooded eyes though, by the way he gnawed at his lip, he too was excited by our revelations.

I walked over to the small table to refill my wine glass. I could sense the excitement of both my companions but I wondered where my conclusions and information would take me. I was tired of it all. I was as much a prisoner here, more comfortable, but still as captive as if I were in the Montmartre prison. I was also tired of the two men behind me. Both of them were actors and I sensed the plot which they controlled was reaching its climax. They did control both it and me, never once had I met anyone else, the Regent Orleans or any notable courtier. No one, that is, except the Abbé Fleury. I had been wary of the priest but now he seemed a safe enough harbour. Perhaps, I wondered, it was time for Old Croft to prepare for a hasty departure. I had established that the Man in the Iron Mask was Eustace D'Auger, soldier, poisoner, blasphemer. A man who had immersed himself in the murky politics of the Paris underworld. D'Auger had probably been arrested with the other prisoners but he had discovered the great secret about how he and the king had the same father. Perhaps he had tried to use this to blackmail Louis XIV and the king, unwilling to execute his half-brother, had him shut away so D'Auger could never babble about his secrets. Indeed that answered the question, why hadn't Louis XIV had the masked man killed? I remembered Maurepas wryly commenting how Louis XIV had adored his mother. Indeed, that may have saved D'Auger, Louis being unable to kill a man who shared his blood and came from the same womb as he. But that was years ago. What would happen now? How would the French crown look after those who discovered dreadful secrets about its past? What chances for an English forger? The Regent's pardon and amnesty were useful but they were no guarantee of true salvation. Behind me D'Estivet moved over, muttering something in Maurepas' ear. Perhaps it was time to make the first moves in arranging my escape. I looked around at the dusty, dirty paintings brought from Madame D'Auger's house.

"Monsieur Maurepas," I called out. "If you are finished with these, perhaps they can be taken back. Who knows, Madame D'Auger may be so grateful to re-possess her property, we might learn something fresh." I smiled as sweetly as possible. "You have my word, I will not try to escape."

"I cannot go with him," D'Estivet observed crossly. "I have other business to attend to."

"Perhaps Ralph," Maurepas interrupted smoothly, "is quite capable of returning the pictures." He smiled just as sweetly back at me. "After all, he will be accompanied by a trooper and the sergeant from the Swiss Guards. Anyway, I am sure our English friend, now we have found the truth, does not want to lose his just rewards."

Those words made me shiver. I thought about Marie. Would it be useful to make an appeal to her? Her father was under her influence. Surely she would wonder if something happened to me and, if given warning, might try to help.

9

I WAS pleased, however, to be out of the Louvre Palace. The pictures were taken down by sweating, cursing troopers from the Swiss Guard and flung into one cart outside a small postern gate of the palace. A Swiss sergeant, small and squat, his red shiny face adorned with a luxurious moustache, walked alongside the driver; at the tail of the cart one of the Swiss Guard strolled aimlessly, hat cocked over his eyes, his musket slung across his shoulder. The driver was no more interesting, dirty, unkempt, an ostler from the palace stables. He seemed as slow and as lazy as the horse he was guiding, pausing now and again to turn and spit. The Swiss sergeant would stop and glare up at him. The fellow smiled insolently back, and our little procession continued, pushing its way through the crowded streets.

We arrived at Madame D'Auger's house and this time she answered the door herself.

"I will not be long," I said to the guard.

"All right," he muttered, warning me with his eyes. I slipped past him and followed the old lady down the dusty passageway. Madame D'Auger ushered me into her 'salon', a cleaner, more tastefully furnished room than the chamber we had last met in. She poured me the smallest glass of wine I had ever seen and flounced down into a great chair, her thin, vein-rimmed hands fluttering like birds over her dowdy, grimy skirts.

"You may sit, Monsieur," she said, indicating a small foot-rest. I squatted down like a boy. I did not mind, courtesy cost so little. Anyway, I like old ladies, especially the eccentricity of this one, though my stomach churned when I saw the decaying body of a rat beneath a wooden chest standing against the far wall.

"You have not brought your friend," Madame D'Auger murmured, "the killer." Her shrewd eyes held mine. "He is a killer, isn't he? I saw the fight. The swords clashing in the air." She smiled primly as if congratulating herself.

"I watched it from my window. A killer," she continued. "Fancy murdering his friends!"

"What do you mean?" I asked.

The old lady's mouth drooped.

"Oh, don't you know? Bernard does. Bernard sees everything. He glimpsed your friend the previous day." She leaned over, her eyes wide. "The day before you came. What's your friend's name?"

"Captain D'Estivet."

"Yes," she said triumphantly. "Bernard saw D'Estivet. He was standing at the corner of the street with the same three men he would kill the next day. He was talking and laughing with them." Madame D'Auger gave a small laugh.

231

"A strange man."

I sat shocked. Why, I asked myself? Why had D'Estivet been meeting those men? He said he didn't know them yet he had arranged a mock fight in which all three had died. A terrible coldness gripped my innards as I reckoned with the cruel depths of D'Estivet's soul. He had lured those men to their deaths. But why? Why such evil?

"Monsieur?"

I looked up at Madame D'Auger.

"D'Estivet," she continued, "your friend, he reminds me of my brother Eustace. A restless, murderous soul. You know, when I was young, I went to see the King's menagerie at Versailles." She patted her white hair. "When I was young, dressed in silks and satins, and the young men ogled me. Anyway," she murmured, half lost in her own thoughts, "I saw a wild cat, a panther I think they call it, in one of the royal cages. Black as night it was with yellow, fiery eyes. It padded silently up and down its cage. You could almost feel the blood pounding in its head. D'Estivet reminds me of that animal, just like Eustace. No peace, no serenity."

Perhaps then I guessed, intuitively, that D'Auger was not the Man in the Iron Mask. Everything I had learnt about the prisoner suggested he was calm, even gentle. I was going to ask Madame D'Auger about her brother but she waved her hand to indicate I was not to interrupt.

"Eustace was evil," she continued. "That's why they put him in a cage."

"A cage?" I interrupted.

"Oh, yes, didn't I tell you? The asylum at St Lazare." Her words clashed like swords in the dry air of that dusty, death-tinged room.

I put my wine glass down, frightened I would drop it.

"Madame," I said, "your brother, Eustace, in a lunatic asylum. But . . . "

"But nothing!" she shrilled. "He was an evil man. I know that. He should have died in the galleys or on the gallows but King Louis XIV, God bless him, had great affection for our mother, so Eustace was imprisoned for life in the asylum of St Lazare."

"Madame," I insisted, "that cannot be!"

"Oh, yes, it was," she snapped back. "Eustace was involved with that evil lot, de Brinvilliers, Belot and the other poisoners. He was arrested and put away." She drew back in her chair, angry at my disbelief. "I can prove it!"

She got up and walked over to the old chest, opened it and, mumbling and groaning, she bent over, her back and joints creaked in protest, as she rummaged amongst the contents. She took out a sheet of yellow parchment and handed it to me. I do not have it now. I cannot recall the full text so I will repeat what I remember. It was dated the 20th June 1678 and sent from the asylum of St Lazare.

"My dear sister," it began, "if you only knew how I suffer. I have no doubt at all that you would do your utmost to get me out of this cruel persecution and captivity in which I have been kept under pretext for ten years . . . I beg you to do all that you judge necessary for my liberty and for my affairs, even if it means approaching the King."

I sat and stared in disbelief. Everything we had worked for was crashing in ruins. Eustace D'Auger must have disappeared into the lunatic house at least one year before the Masked Man was arrested. Only one thing remained. King Louis XIV and his ministers had used Eustace's name as a further veil of secrecy around their famous prisoner. I looked up at Madame D'Auger.

"What happened?" I said.

She handed me a second piece of paper.

"Oh, the king was quite angry," she observed. "Go on, read it!"

The second letter was easy to memorise. I think it read as follows:

"Missive from the King to the

General Superior of the House of St Lazare. This comes in the name of the King himself. Dearly beloved, we are writing this letter to tell you that it is our intention that Monsieur D'Auger should have no communication with anyone, not even his sister . . . Let this be done without fail. This is our desire — 17th August 1678."

I meekly handed the letter back as the Swiss sergeant opened the door.

"Oh, get out!" I snarled. "Get out, now!"

The man took one look at my face and hastily withdrew. I turned back to Madame D'Auger, took her hand and kissed it gently.

"Madame," I said, "I thank you. I would like to tell you what all this means, but I dare not."

The old lady smiled as if I were merely commenting on the quality of her wine. I went out to the sergeant.

"Look, man," I said, "I want no protests. Go back to the Louvre Palace, tell Monsieur Maurepas and Captain D'Estivet that I must see them on a matter of grave urgency in the Café Procope. It's most urgent. I will wait there until they come."

The sergeant shook his head.

"I can't leave you, sir. I have my orders."

"If you don't do as I say," I hissed, "you will be cleaning stables for the next five years! Leave your trooper with me. Give him instructions to guard me, but go!"

The sergeant looked as if he was going to refuse but thought better of it and hurried down the passageway calling the trooper to come in.

"Stay with him!" he barked. "Wherever he goes, you go! If he tries to escape, shoot the bastard's head off!"

He scurried off. I bade farewell to the startled Madame D'Auger who had followed me out, begging her to keep the letters, and hastened into the street. The carter still sat there. He grinned wickedly down at me and my gormless guard.

"Monsieur would like a lift?" he asked.

I looked up. A cold breeze blew. I glanced down the street to where D'Estivet had killed the three assassins.

"Yes," I said, "you know the Café Procope?"

"Near the Bastille?"

I nodded and the carter flicked his whip as the trooper and I climbed in. We trundled over the cobbles, down narrow alleyways and on to the broad thoroughfare leading up to the Bastille. We drew strange looks but I didn't care and the trooper seemed pleased to be able to rest. Not the most vigilant sentry, he was half asleep by the time we reached the Café Procope. I told him to stand on guard outside and entered the warm darkness. A slattern served brandy and coffee and I sipped them absent mindedly, thinking over what I had learnt. D'Estivet was up to some villainy, but what? And why?

And if D'Auger was not the masked man then who was? I jumped as a shadow came alongside me. The carter stood there, a brimming glass of wine in his hand.

"May I join you, Monsieur?" he asked, and sat down before I could reply.

I studied the man uneasily. He was dirty, unkempt, but his eyes were clear and sharp, and his hands, though stained with dirt, were soft and well manicured.

"Monsieur," I began, "I suspect you are not here to while away a few hours, just as I think that you do not drive a cart round Paris most of the time. So what do you want?"

The fellow put down his glass.

"My name is Salinet. I work for the Abbé Fleury. I bring some warnings."

"I have had them before."

"I also bring information," he added quickly. "I will tell you a story."

I shrugged.

"I have heard a few already, Monsieur.

So what's yours?"

"First, Monsieur, the warnings. The Abbé Fleury says that the net is closing in as you near the end of your usefulness. You must be very careful. If you plan escape, and the Abbé thinks you do, tell him first. He will help you."

I smiled, as if the silly bastards thought I was such an innocent. Of course, I knew the end was in sight though I was slightly perturbed how a priest, who had only met me once, could read my thoughts.

"Go on!" I said.

"We know," the fellow replied, "as do many people, that the masked man was arrested in 1669. I would like to take you back a year earlier, to April 1668, and an agent, an arch-plotter, named Claude Roux. Have you ever heard of him? You haven't? Well, Roux was a spy, a republican, well known to the authorities in London, Paris and Geneva. He served your Cromwell as a secret agent but got himself a pardon from Charles II by providing the English crown with a list of his fellow spies."

"A man after my own heart," I commented.

Salinet smiled.

"Roux was superb at his job. He could double-cross, plot, and betray but finally he found a true cause, working for a secret organisation in Geneva called the Committee of Ten, dedicated to the overthrow of Louis XIV. Indeed, such a nuisance did Roux become, that both the secret services of Louis XIV and Charles II spent time and money trying to ensnare him. In May 1669 Roux was finally captured. On the 25th May Louis XIV wrote to the French ambassador in London announcing Roux's capture. Louis instructed him to deliver the news in person to Charles II and his ministers, observing their faces carefully for any signs of discomfort or alarm.

"How do you know all this?" I asked.

The fellow shrugged.

"I merely repeat what the Abbé has told me." He grinned. "If you think I am lying, look at the index of royal letters. We know Monsieur Maurepas has access to them. It is just a matter of what you are looking for, isn't it?"

"Go on!" I said.

"The French Authorities interrogated Roux. The one thing they did learn was that Roux had a valet in London, a Frenchman called Martin. On the 20th June Roux tried to commit suicide; using a broken knife he slashed his genitals but this was discovered in time. The next day Roux stood trial, was found guilty and condemned to death. He was executed soon afterwards, broken on the wheel."

"So," I said. "How is Roux so important?"

"Ah. For two reasons. First, no one ever found out who this Committee of Ten in Switzerland was. Secondly, Roux's valet, Martin, seemed very important to him and to the French authorities. The French government first tried to bribe Martin to return to Paris and then strove to get him extradited."

Salinet fell quiet, sipping from his wine glass.

"And what happened then?"

The fellow looked at me.

"Nothing. Nothing at all. But Monsieur Abbé proposes two things. First, what happened to that valet? Secondly, and this is most important, you must ask Monsieur Maurepas to have a meeting with the Regent and demand to see the letters of Queen Anne, mother of Louis XIV. These letters are hidden away under secret seal, they are written in code. No one is given access to them. Monsieur Abbé thinks they will tell you all you need to know."

"So, I ask for the letters of Queen Anne?"

"Yes, for the years 1644 – 1649. Ask for them through Maurepas. He will also tell you what happened at the court during those years." The spy clenched his fist round the wine cup. "But you must ask for these letters."

I sipped at my own drink. I realised the story of Roux and his valet Martin were connected with the masked man. But who was Martin? And did the title 'valet' signify anything? King Louis XIV had used this term to describe the masked prisoner. And the Regent? Was he, the Duke of Orleans, the secret Grand Master of the Knights Templar? The deeper I got into this mystery the more I wondered why he wanted to know. I asked Salinet this. He just smirked and looked away.

"Don't you know?" he slyly asked. "Our Regent does not live for the intricacies of politics. His brain has been, is, and always will be in his codpiece. They say he is hot after some woman and she has refused his advances till he gives her the name of the masked man." The spy lowered his voice and leaned closer. "They say it's his daughter," he whispered. "What do you think of that?" He straightened up. "Do not tell Maurepas what I have said," he continued. "Just tell him you need the letters. Say," he looked up at the yellow stained ceiling, "say you have learnt something from Madame D'Auger. A great secret which only these letters will reveal. Maurepas will believe that. Remember, Madame D'Auger's mother was a favourite lady-in-waiting to the Queen."

"Why," I asked, "are these letters so important?"

Salinet's face lapsed back into its silly grin. He leaned across, waving a dirty finger in my face.

"I tell you, Monsieur." His voice rose. "The women of Paris are more beautiful and know more tricks than . . . "

Salinet's eyes slid away and I felt a chill run down my spine. I had been so engrossed with Salinet, the room was so comfortable, quiet and warm,

I had forgotten to look around. When I did, Maurepas and D'Estivet were standing there glaring furiously at me. I stared back. Salinet just slipped out, bowing and touching his forelock. My companions let him through without a second glance and joined me at the table.

"Well, Ralph," Maurepas smiled like an indulgent schoolteacher, "we received your message. Our apologies for the delay but Captain D'Estivet was engaged elsewhere." He looked furtively at the soldier, who merely shrugged and called across the maid to bring some drinks.

"How is Marie?" I asked.

"Oh, she is well. She sends you her good wishes. I think she misses you." Maurepas smiled slyly but D'Estivet refused to rise to the veiled taunt. "Ralph," Maurepas continued, "you have news? We received your urgent message."

"Eustace D'Auger," I replied, "he is not our man. He is not the masked prisoner. Oh, he was locked away all right, but not in prison but in the madhouse at Saint Lazare."

I thought even then, for a moment, they were not surprised, more expectant, as if waiting for something else. They sat and heard me out as I described my visit to Madame D'Auger.

"What else?" Maurepas asked when I had finished. "What else did you learn, Ralph?"

"Ah," I controlled my excitement. "I know something else but, to pursue it to the finish, I need certain letters." I paused. "Letters of Queen Anne, mother of Louis XIV." I paused as if trying to recollect the dates. "Letters for the years 1644 – 1649."

I watched Maurepas intently. Had he expected this? Was it excitement, fear or anger which flared in his eyes? D'Estivet looked away, quietly beating a tattoo on the table with his fingers.

"This is feckless," the soldier commented. "We have found the masked man, Eustace D'Auger. The

Regent knows that. Let us have done with it!"

D'Estivet, however, refused to meet my eyes. Did he suspect that I had seen through his game? I had this irresistible urge to confront both of them, to scream my questions at them. I knew why the Regent, Duke of Orleans, wanted the secret. He was a roué who wanted to lift the lacy petticoats of some lady. But what did these two want? They saw some profit in this for themselves and not just the thanks of a prince. What was the secret order of the Templars? Were they members? Both of them or just D'Estivet? And why had the Captain arranged that deadly duel? I kept silent, took a deep breath and sipped the fiery brandy D'Estivet had ordered.

"Captain D'Estivet," I said, "you must believe me. I have seen the letters. If we tried to insist that D'Auger was the masked man then all our work would come to nothing." I glared at him. "Can't you understand? I have actually seen the royal warrant that D'Auger be kept at Saint Lazare for life!"

Maurepas took me warmly by the hand as if I were an old friend.

"Ralph," he beseeched, "I beg you, give me a few moments with Captain D'Estivet."

I did what he asked, standing at the entrance of the drinking-house staring into the darkness. Outside, the trooper leaned half asleep against the wall. Maurepas must have asked him to stay; remembering the assault on D'Estivet and myself, I was glad. There was no sign of Salinet and I idly wondered why he and the Abbé Fleury were so interested in what I was doing. I looked over my shoulder. D'Estivet and Maurepas were sitting, heads together, even an innocent child would have described them as conspirators. The archivist was whispering in his companion's ear. I glanced away. A few minutes later. they joined me, Maurepas clapping me affectionately on the shoulder.

We left the café and made our way back to the Louvre Palace with the trooper dispiritedly trailing behind us. It was a cool evening, not a cloud in the sky, so the stars seemed like a web of jewels sparkling against the velvet darkness. I wondered if I would ever return to England and how I could get out of the trap I was in. Would my companions help? Or discard me as they would an old rag?

"What are you thinking about, Ralph?" Maurepas asked.

"Anne of Austria," I lied. "I believe the secret of the masked man is connected with her. Tell me about her."

"A Spaniard," he answered. "She married Louis XIII when she was fourteen. If there was ever a marriage made in hell, then hers was it. Anne's husband was small, nervous, ungainly, with very few real virtues. He was not a ruler but depended on two churchmen, Cardinal Richelieu and, when he died,

Cardinal Mazarin. Anne was different. She was beautiful, passionate and impetuous. Her name was linked with many men." The archivist paused and adjusted his cloak. "No one really knows," he continued, "the true nature of her relationship with her husband. I tell you this," he said, "Anne of Austria was pregnant a number of times and suffered several miscarriages. Unlike D'Estivet and others, I do not believe Louis XIII was incapable of begetting children. He may have had difficulty. He may not have been attracted to the pleasures of the bed," he smiled slyly at me, "as you are, Englishman. But he did his conjugal duty."

"Anne outlived her husband?" I asked.

"Yes, yes," the archivist replied. "In 1642 Cardinal Richelieu died. The following year Louis XIV followed him to the grave and affairs of state fell firmly into the hands of Anne, who became Queen Regent, and Richelieu's protegé, the Italian cardinal Mazarin.

These two ruled the country for the next twenty years despite opposition, even civil war." Maurepas stopped and stared down at the ground. "You know," he continued softly, "Fouquet, who was incarcerated in the same prison as the masked man, was one of Mazarin's henchmen."

"When did Mazarin die?"

"Oh," Maurepas furrowed his brow in concentration, "in 1661. The same year Fouquet was arrested."

"And Anne of Austria?" I asked.

"She died five years later."

"You think Anne holds the secret, don't you?" D'Estivet suddenly asked.

I nodded and we walked on in silence. At the Louvre Palace some party of official reception was being held. The courtyards were full of coaches, grooms, ostlers. Inside the rooms were bathed in the light of thousands of candles. The corridors glowed like polished glass and the air was heavy with the warm fragrance of perfume and the soft early smells of spring. Footmen, flunkies and servants, resplendent in blue and gold livery, scurried along corridors, lined with guardsmen dressed in full regimental paraphernalia. Maurepas led us past them into the great ballroom. Musicians in the gallery above played softly to a room packed with beautiful people, dancing, talking, eating; men in gorgeous military uniforms, ladies in silks of every hue. None of them spared us a glance as we forced our way through the throng up to the great dais where the Regent, dressed in deep purple silk, sat on a jewel-encrusted, silver throne under a huge scarlet canopy.

The Regent slouched like some spoilt boy, his old, dissipated face coated with a thick white powder. His lips were painted a carmine red and beauty spots in the shape of hearts had been placed along his cheek bones. He looked the most lecherous rogue I had ever clapped eyes on. He sat staring moodily at the throng. Beside him, sitting on a smaller chair, sat a young woman in her thirties; there was a faint family resemblance, the dissolute face, large eyes and patrician nose. I guessed she must be the Regent's daughter, the one he lusted after. I stared at her curiously as Maurepas, ordering us to stay, approached the throne, bowed lower than I had ever seen him do, before whispering urgently in the Regent's ear. At first the Duke just lolled there but then his eyes snapped up. He stared at me, nodding imperceptibly as Maurepas spoke. When the archivist finished, the Regent nodded, muttered a few words, got up and walked behind the throne. A servant pulled back the arras and, following Maurepas' urgent signals, we stepped on to the dais and followed the Regent into a small chamber. No servants were there. Maurepas, taking a tinder, lit the great six-branched candelabra on the table whilst the Regent made himself comfortable in the room's one and only chair. There was no ceremony or court etiquette here. The Duke came swiftly to the point.

"You want to see the letters of Anne of Austria, Englishman?" he snapped. "Why?"

"I asked Monsieur Maurepas for them," I answered quickly, feverishly wondering what explanation I could give.

"I know that," the Regent replied. "But why do you want to see them? No one understands them. They are written in code."

"Your Grace," I stuttered, "I know something. I have a key which can unlock the mystery you want solved. I believe I can do it in days. Perhaps even sooner. I do not know what I am looking for but," I laughed nervously, "I will only find it when I see it."

The Regent ran his finger along his lower lip, ensuring the paint there was still smooth and clear.

"These letters," he replied, "like the personal letters of any prince, are not for the vulgar or baseborn to study and laugh about." He straightened in his chair. "You are talking, sir, about my own grandmother."

"Your Grace," I snapped swiftly. "I understand. You may well refuse these letters to be handed over but, if that is so, the mystery will never be solved."

The Regent merely stared at me. Somehow or other he had the same eyes as D'Estivet, Villon, even the Abbé Fleury, hard and clear, as if a presence lurked behind them, some demon which understood one's thoughts. The Regent glanced round the chamber and smiled thinly. Sweet heaven, I knew what the old bastard was thinking. He was about to hand those letters over but whether I would be allowed to go free, pardon or not, would be another matter. The Regent stood up, dusting flecks of dust from the sleeve of his purple jacket.

"You may have the letters," he drawled. "They will be in the library tomorrow. You, Englishman, will be allowed to study them." He walked closer to me and stroked me along my cheek. I could smell his rotten breath beneath the wine fumes but I did not flinch. "I gave you a pardon, Englishman, an amnesty. I am now giving you the privilege of looking at a Queen's letters, you, an English forger." He waved one elegant finger under my nose. Now, Monsieur Croft, you must earn your pay. Do you understand?"

I stared back. He smiled, his mood suddenly changing. He tweaked my cheek and, brushing by me, returned to his festivities in the great ballroom beyond.

There were two musketeers waiting for us outside the library when we returned there. Maurepas and D'Estivet questioned me once more about D'Auger, bade me goodnight and handed me over to the custody of the two soldiers who escorted me back to my chamber. They stood guard there all night as I lay tossing on the bed wondering what I should do. I knew I had lied. All I had discovered was that D'Auger was not the masked man. All I could trust were my own wits, perhaps I would stumble on something in the letters of Anne of Austria which would resolve this matter once and for all.

10

THE next morning Maurepas and D'Estivet took me back to the library. Another royal official joined us, a tall, angular, stoop-backed man, who introduced himself as Monsieur Clovell, chief notary and secretary to the Duke of Orleans. He brought a small, wooden casket which contained Anne of Austria's letters. The box was ordinary enough, made of stained wood, reinforced with steel bands: it had three locks and a royal seal. Clovell broke this and, using a special key, released the three clasps. He tipped back the lid and pushed the entire casket under my nose. The faint smell of perfume, a mixture of rose water and sandalwood, took me back down the years to the beautiful, passionate woman who penned the letters which had curled and yellowed at the bottom of the casket.

"I am here at His Grace's request," Clovell announced. "His Grace the Duke of Orleans is most insistent, only the Englishman is allowed to look at these letters. Monsieur Maurepas and Captain D'Estivet, you are welcome to stay but I must insist you are not to handle any of the late Queen's correspondence." He smiled wearily, "I, of course, will remain here all the time."

Maurepas shrugged graciously and moved away. D'Estivet picked at his teeth angrily, one hand falling to the scabbard of his sword; I believe the murderous bastard would have liked to run Monsieur Clovell through the innards there and then.

So, I commenced my task. I took out each letter and studied it most carefully, Clovell informing me that I had only received the letters for the years I had asked. At first, I could find nothing. Many of the letters were simply notes, private memoranda, all the normal missives between any high-born lady and an ever-increasing circle of friends, admirers and clients. Some, however, were different. Oh, they appeared innocent enough on the surface. In these the Queen came across as a very garrulous and witty woman but the letters were vague. There were references to certain animals, plants; these, of course, were the letters written in code. I divided the contents of the casket into two piles, those not worth bothering about and those written in the secret cipher. After a while I was able to concentrate on this latter group. Some of the codes and ciphers were easy to understand, the Queen apparently enjoying herself, writing innocent notes, baiting those who intercepted her correspondence in order to trap her. A small group of letters, however, were very long and conveyed the Queen's passion and deep longings. They were addressed to no one in particular but, beneath the secret code and cipher, they conveyed news about people and happenings the Queen felt deeply about. All these letters were dated after 1643, the year her husband, Louis XIII, died.

Now, I am a good forger. I can boast that any letter, whatever the cipher, will eventually give up its secrets, but these proved difficult. The days passed in monotonous tension. I would begin work in the morning and study the documents until late in the evening. The hours of the day were marked by the sound of cannon fire from the royal parks, the tolling of a bell or the soft shuffle as servants came in to light fires or candles or to serve meals. The presence of my three companions increased the tension: D'Estivet pacing up and down as if guarding some battlement; Maurepas sitting in a chair, making his own notes; and Monsieur Clovell, who seemed to live in a world of his own, carrying on his own normal palace duties whilst keeping an ever vigilant eye on me. At night when I had finished, my head and eyes ached with the strain. Clovell would gather the documents up again, put them back in the casket and remove them as a priest would the sacred vessels from the altar. Naturally, Maurepas and D'Estivet would question me but I could tell them very little and I would stumble back to my own chamber to lie in the refreshing darkness while my tired brain tried to sort out the jumble of facts.

I thought of Marie and wondered if Maurepas would arrange another of his dinner parties. I hinted the same to him, and on the Friday of the week I had started studying the Queen's correspondence, he graciously invited D'Estivet and myself to what he termed one of his 'little suppers'. It proved to be a splendid and sumptuous occasion. Marie was as beautiful as ever; dressed in a dark red velvet dress caught tightly around her waist and fastened high at the neck. She looked magnificent, her hair piled high on her head, the light of the candle catching the pure lucid quality of her skin and those dark lustrous eyes which spoke as eloquently as any love poem.

Looking back on that evening I will always remember her as she was then. I liked to think she dressed for me but perhaps D'Estivet, too, was intended for her silken web. The meal was sumptuous, the dishes so varied and tasty I was tempted to break my resolve and ask how one woman could prepare such an array of dishes, but I kept quiet. I just sat, happy to be out of that library, no longer locked in the passionate but secret correspondence of a long-dead queen. Maurepas was courteous and charming, D'Estivet, surly and withdrawn, only relaxing and mellowing when Marie smiled on him. Naturally, the conversation turned back to our task. Under the influence of wine I described the letters I had studied, remarking on how they said a great deal but actually told me very little. When the table had been cleared and Marie herself had served us coffee and liqueurs, Maurepas leaned over and asked,

"Ralph, whom do these letters mention the most?"

"No one in particular," I replied.

The archivist licked his lips.

"Let us take another path then. Whom do you think they should mention the most?"

Despite the good wine and my sense of well-being, the agitation and despair of my fruitless search returned, as if death itself clasped me by the shoulder, its skeletal hand sending shivers of fear down my spine. The letters had revealed nothing. Perhaps it was time to tell the truth. I put my brandy glass down.

"Monsieur Maurepas, the letters have yielded nothing," I took a deep breath. "To quote Shakespeare 'Nothing can come of nothing.' Perhaps it is my ignorance of the times but whom should I be looking for?"

"Only one man," he commented, "was very close to the widowed Anne of Austria, the Roman Catholic priest." I noticed how the archivist almost spat the title out. "The Roman Catholic prelate, Cardinal Mazarin!"

"Tell me more about him," I said.

"Mazarin was an Italian," Maurepas replied. He grinned at D'Estivet. "He became a captain in the papal army but he excelled as a diplomat so the Pope sent him to France."

"When was that?" I asked.

Maurepas rubbed his chin.

"I looked at my file of dates recently, it was about 1631. He stayed in France, becoming Richelieu's right-hand man. In 1641 he was made a cardinal and a year later, when Richelieu died, Chief Minister of France, a post he continued to hold after Louis XIII's death in 1643. Mazarin brought his family with him to Paris: the Mancini girls, they became famous courtesans at the court of Charles II in England, and of course his other relations, the Martinozzis or Martinots as they were called in France. Why do you ask?"

I shrugged, hiding my flicker of excitement at something he had said.

"Look," I replied. "Monsieur, you mentioned a paper, a list of dates. Could you provide me with that?"

Maurepas agreed and the conversation passed on to lighter, more superficial matters. I heard a clock chime in the hallway, and Maurepas tactfully indicated I should leave, saying that Captain D'Estivet would be a safe enough escort back to the Louvre. I kissed Marie's hand (I could swear she pressed mine that little bit tighter), and D'Estivet morosely took me back along narrow, winding streets to the Louvre. He hardly uttered a word. At the Palace gates, however, he grasped me by the arm and forced me to look at him.

"I don't like you, Englishman!" he grated. "You should never have been involved in this matter. I don't trust you and I would be grateful if, where Monsieur Maurepas' daughter is concerned, you would keep your thoughts to yourself!" He preened himself like a peacock. "I shall tell as much to Marie when I see her later this evening." He smiled at the surprise in my eyes. "Oh, yes, Englishman, the evening may be over for you, but not for me."

He turned, cloak swinging, and swaggered off. Perhaps it was the wine, his hectoring ways, but my anger spilled out.

"D'Estivet!" I shouted.

He continued to walk on.

"D'Estivet! Are you one of the secret Templars?"

Oh, I enjoyed that. The bastard came back, hands falling to that bloody sword. I stepped hastily back to the gateway so the sentry at the far door could see us. D'Estivet would not draw his weapon in the precincts of the royal palace.

"What did you say, Englishman?"

"I asked if you were a member of the Secret Order of the Templars."

In the faint light of the torches, I

could see D'Estivet's face was white and a muscle high in his cheek twitched with anger.

"You make their sign," I coolly added.

"No, Englishman," he answered, "I am not a Templar." He stepped closer. "But perhaps you are. Maybe that is why you are here now and not swinging on the end of some gibbet or keeping your friends, the rats, company at the bottom of the Bastille!" He wagged a fist in front of my nose. "But soon, Englishman, the hunt will be over and, if the Regent doesn't settle with you, I will!" He turned and sauntered off into the darkness.

I spent the week-end a prisoner in my chamber at the Louvre. The usual guards appeared, ever vigilant; where I went they always followed. Of course, no work was done, so Monsieur Clovell did not bring the casket of the Queen's letters to me. Maurepas, too, was involved in his own affairs, or so I thought. He appeared late on Saturday evening, an anxious look on his face, asking me if I had seen Captain D'Estivet. I curtly told him I had not. Maurepas nodded and stalked off. I wandered round the palace, ogling the occasional serving girl or chambermaid but somehow or other, everyone in the palace seemed to know my true station and I was avoided.

On Sunday morning, as I was strolling in one of the courtyards, the Abbé Fleury passed me. He stopped and smiled, making a soothing movement with his hand. God knows what he was trying to communicate. Sometimes I glimpsed Salinet. He would appear as if from nowhere, tidier, more genteel than the last time we met. He, too, just smiled secretively and passed on. For the rest, I spent my time thinking about that small nugget of information Monsieur Maurepas had given me. Something he had said struck a chord in my memory, something I had seen in the letters of Queen Anne. By Monday morning I was so impatient I almost grabbed the casket out of Clovell's hands and began work immediately. Clovell murmured wonderingly whether we should wait for Monsieur Maurepas and Captain D'Estivet. I snarled back my reply so he decided to let me be and took his usual seat, lost in his own work.

I did not find a solution that morning and it must have been about noon before I missed Maurepas. I needed him because he had promised to hand over the file of dates, listing the main events of Queen Anne's life. Bells sounded, clocks chimed, a servant brought some bread and wine for me and my companion. I was sipping from my glass when I heard a tremendous commotion outside and Maurepas (a consummate actor if there ever was one) burst white-faced, wide-eyed into the room.

"Croft!" he called, ignoring the startled Clovell. "You are to come now! I mean now!"

I followed him out of the room. He

ran down the stairs as agile as a young boy, into the main hallway and down another staircase into the palace cellars; a row of dark, dungeon-like rooms. One of these, however, was now well lit by torches of pitch fixed in niches in the wall. The room was empty except for a pallet of wood now covered with a dirty white sheet stained with blood.

"It's D'Estivet!" Maurepas murmured.

He pulled back the sheet. D'Estivet was lying there, a great red black wound just under his heart. The clothes he wore were dirty and blood-splattered. D'Estivet was no Adonis in life, in death he looked truly dreadful. His eyes, wide open, stared sightlessly up into the darkness. His lips parted, in the rictus of death, gave his white, twisted face a gruesome look as if he were still smirking at me. The gloves on his hands had been white the last time I had seen them. Now they were filthy, stained with his own blood and the muck and dirt of where he had been tossed. The wound, when I examined it more closely, was more a ragged rent as if someone had run a sword or dagger through and violently twisted it.

"He's still wearing his sword," I murmured.

"What is that?" Maurepas asked.

"His sword," I repeated. "Look! He's still wearing it."

"Which means?" Maurepas asked.

"Well," I muttered, "D'Estivet was a brilliant swordsman but he lies dead, not killed with a bullet or stabbed in the back but in the chest. Whoever killed him must have been quick. Surely D'Estivet would have drawn his sword as soon as anyone approached, especially someone armed."

Maurepas made a grimace with his lips.

"Perhaps he did," he commented. "And the assassin put it back."

I leaned over the body, my hand touched the thigh of the dead man, it felt cold and hard under my hand and I realised D'Estivet must have been dead at least a day. Gently I pulled out that dreadful sword but the blade shone like glass. I shoved it back in again.

"If D'Estivet drew his sword," I wryly commented, "then whoever returned it took great care to clean and polish it."

Maurepas spread his hands.

"Perhaps D'Estivet was surprised," he said. "Perhaps someone was waiting for him. It's happened before. A well-known assassin's trick to wait round a corner with a dagger or sword and let your enemy simply walk upon it."

"Perhaps," I replied, scrutinising the scabbard and belt D'Estivet wore. There was something wrong but I did not care. I was glad that the bastard was dead, one less danger to threaten me. Moreover, I reasoned, a man like D'Estivet must have his enemies. Who knows, perhaps even friends or companions of the three bravados he had lured to their deaths in the Rue des Bons Enfants.

"What happened?" I asked.

Maurepas sat on a small stone plinth,

wiping the sweat from his brow with the hem of his cloak.

"After D'Estivet accompanied you back to the Louvre Palace," he began, "you remember, last Friday?"

I nodded.

"He returned to our house. We drank some more brandy. D'Estivet left in the early hours but agreed to return later in the day to discuss certain matters. He never came so I went looking for him. You remember I asked you. When was it?"

"Saturday evening," I replied, watching the archivist carefully.

"On Sunday when he failed to arrive, I went to the Palace," Maurepas continued, "a search was made of the morgues and hospitals. D'Estivet's body was found in the mortuary of St Jerome. The Regent sent me to identify the corpse. I learnt from the attendants there that D'Estivet's corpse had been brought in on one of the death carts."

Maurepas, his face white, his skin

glistening with sweat, looked over at D'Estivet's corpse. I thought he was going to vomit but he just got up and pulled the sheet roughly back over his dead companion's face.

"It would seem," he continued, "that D'Estivet's body was found in a small alleyway on a midden heap behind the cathedral of Notre Dame. His purse had been taken and any documents which may have borne his name."

"But not his sword," I wondered.

Maurepas turned his head and spat.

"Of course not!" he brusquely replied. "A man like D'Estivet carries his own personal sword. No ruffian would dare wear or try to sell it. It would be a virtual admission of guilt." Maurepas smiled sourly. "However, I agree with you, Ralph. D'Estivet was killed suddenly, or overwhelmed by a gang of ruffians. One held him whilst another drove a sword or dagger into his chest." Maurepas shrugged. "I had a carter bring the body here. D'Estivet having no family, the Regent has agreed to hold a quiet military funeral in the church of St Paul's. Rather fitting don't you think to be buried in the same graveyard as the masked prisoner?"

I smiled. Who cared where the sod went?

"Oh," Maurepas got up and came towards me. "I know you are not unhappy at D'Estivet's death. In fact," he continued softly, "D'Estivet had sworn that whatever the Regent said, he would personally ensure your death."

"He was a bastard!" I replied. "He liked killing. Perhaps," I decided to be a little braver and test the archivist, "perhaps he was killed by the Secret Order of the Templars."

Maurepas stepped back in astonishment. "D'Estivet, one of those!" he gasped. "One of those plotters, secret revolutionaries!" He shook his head. "No, I cannot believe that. D'Estivet was a soldier, a good one, a spy, silent and efficient. One of the most trusted officers of the Regent. Ralph!" he shook his head. "Be most careful what you say. Oh!" he added sharply, "I have a message for you. His Grace the Regent has become most impatient; he has given you one week, one more week to prove that it was necessary to study Queen Anne's letters. So, have you learnt anything?"

"It would help, Monsieur," I snapped back, "if you gave me that document you promised me, the short chronicle of the main events in those years following Louis XIII's death."

Maurepas slid a small scroll of paper from the sleeve of his cloak.

"I had not forgotten, Ralph," he replied. He looked kindly at me.

"What will happen to me, Monsieur Maurepas?" I asked abruptly. "Will the Regent honour his pardon when all this is over?"

"I don't know," he murmured, taking me by the arm and walking me back down the passageway to the main cellar door. "I really don't know."

"Marie?" I asked. "How is she?"

Maurepas smiled thinly.

"You may not believe this, Ralph," he answered quietly, "but Marie liked Captain D'Estivet. She saw something in him perhaps others did not. She is distraught at his death but sends you her kind regards and good wishes. She is glad that you were detained at the Louvre Palace." Maurepas stared at me. "Oh, yes, Ralph, when D'Estivet's body was discovered, even I wondered if you had a hand in his death. Don't look so shocked," he jibed. "You hated him but the guards at the palace gate said they saw D'Estivet leaving you and, of course, you have been kept under close scrutiny ever since."

Maurepas took me back to my own room, murmuring a few words to the musketeer on guard before slipping quietly away. For the first time I was glad that the palace guards kept watch so faithfully; if I had been allowed to wander around at my own whim, I am sure I would have been arrested on suspicion of D'Estivet's murder. I was also a little frightened that whoever killed D'Estivet might also want my death. I reached under my bed and brought out the rapier and pistol the Regent had given me. I ensured that the belt carried two small pouches, one with powder the other with balls. The rapier, too, was serviceable, it would cut and slash like any other. I cleaned and loaded the pistol ready for use and hid the weapons away, hoping I would not have to use them. In any crisis, I prefer to trust my sharp wits and nimble legs.

More at peace, I spent the rest of that day studying the chronicle of events that Maurepas had given me and trying to recall some of the phrases from Anne of Austria's letters. The next morning I wrote out those dates which were significant and kept them firmly in my mind: in 1631, Mazarin first came to Paris; in 1641 he was made a cardinal; in 1642 made a member of Louis XIII's council, taking over absolute power from Richelieu. In 1643 Mazarin was made godfather to the future Louis XIV and on 14th May in the same year Louis XIII died, and Queen Anne became sole Regent with Mazarin as her chief minister. In 1661 Mazarin died and Nicholas Fouquet became chief minister but was suddenly arrested. In 1666 Anne of Austria died and three years later the masked man was arrested. I also listed all I knew about the masked prisoner.

Primo — he was young, tall, athletic, of good physique. Secundo — he was French, of noble birth, a Catholic and could speak English quite well. Tertio, he was held in special prisons where no one except Fouquet spoke to him. Quarto — he was masked whenever he was taken around or allowed to exercise. Quinto — he knew some dreadful secret. Sexto — Louis XIV supervised his custody and imprisonment. Septimo — his death certificate bore the name Marciel.

Once again I went back to Anne of Austria's letters and applied all I now knew. In two days I deciphered her secret code, based on a series of numbers as well as a range of terms or titles. I felt a quiet thrill of triumph that I was the only person, apart from this dead queen, who actually knew to whom and what she was referring. I hid my secret elation from Monsieur Clovell as I proceeded to build a picture in my own mind of who the masked man was, why he had been imprisoned and why Louis XIV had regarded him as such a danger. I spread my net further, demanding the right to consult chronicles and broadsheets of the time. Maurepas suspected my discovery, he could sense the subtle change in mood though he never questioned me.

I spent all my waking hours in that library, reluctant to stop even for a short walk or something to eat. Early on Thursday morning when Maurepas had left to attend D'Estivet's funeral (I could not play the hypocrite so I declined Maurepas invitation to see that murderous bastard off), the Abbé Fleury slipped into the library. He beckoned Monsieur Clovell over and whispered in his ear. At first Clovell protested but Fleury quietly insisted and so the Regent's secretary just shrugged and left the room. Fleury, his robes billowing about him, came across and stood over me.

"So, Englishman," he whispered as if the room were full of spies, "you have found the secret?"

"Who told you that?" I stuttered.

Fleury laughed as he sat down, playing with a huge amethyst ring on one of his fingers. He waved his hand airily about.

"Nothing happens in this palace without the knowledge of Abbé Fleury," he hinted. "I know, Englishman, that I am privileged to sit beside the one living man who knows the true identity of the Man in the Iron Mask. I also suspect that the information you gathered, if published abroad, would cause great scandal to the French crown." He cocked his head sideways. "I am right, am I not?"

"Perhaps. But there are still gaps."

"Such as?"

I stared around as if concerned that there were holes in the walls where people could stand and listen to muttered secrets.

"Englishman, you can tell me."

"Why should I?"

The Abbé Fleury rose and went over to lean against one of the windows, staring down at the courtyard below.

"You should tell me, Englishman, because at this very hour your former colleague, Captain D'Estivet, one of France's finest swordsmen, an officer in the crack corps of musketeers, is being given an official though very quiet burial in St Paul's graveyard." The Abbé played with the great crucifix which hung on a gold chain round his neck. He snapped his fingers. "That," he added, "is what was given for the life of a man like D'Estivet. So, what do you think will happen to you? Why not see me as your friend?" He came over and placed a hand on my shoulder. "Put not your trust in princes," he muttered, quoting from one of the psalms. "Do not trust their letters of pardon but put your trust in myself and God."

And, before I could answer, he slipped softly out of the room.

To be quite honest, I did not give a bugger about Fleury. What concerned me was how I should use the information I had. And how could I get out of France, slip over the border into Holland or perhaps flee east to the German States? I spent that whole evening wondering about whom I could trust. Maurepas and Marie? Or the Abbé Fleury? On Friday morning I made my decision. Later in the day I told Clovell to take the casket away as I no longer needed it. Maurepas called in but I said I needed more time to reflect on what I had learnt. He seemed satisfied and left. I went up to my own chamber and, taking the manuscripts I had gathered and the money the Regent had given me,

I placed them into a leather bag. I told the guard that it was most urgent that I see Monsieur Maurepas and I wanted to go to his house immediately. The fellow protested but I told him he would have to answer to the Regent so he reluctantly agreed. He accompanied me down to the hallway of the palace but I pretended I had forgotten something and, despite his grumbled protests, went back to my chamber and took from beneath the bed the broad, leather belt with its sword and pistol. I took off my cloak and put them on carefully. As I buckled the strap I thought of D'Estivet's corpse and realised what I had seen wrong in that macabre cellar room. Astonished, I sat down on my bed, allowing memories to flood back: little glimpses like pieces in a puzzle which, if kept separate, mean nothing but, if put together, form a complete picture. I heard the guard knock on the door but I ignored him as I tried to control my rising panic. I could not go to Maurepas' house, it was too dangerous, or was it? Again the knock and the door opened.

"Monsieur!" The officer's face was concerned, perhaps he sensed my panic for I felt weak and frightened. My heart was thudding like a drum, my stomach lurched as if I was going to vomit.

"Monsieur, you are all right?" He came into the room.

"Yes, yes!" I replied weakly. "I am all right, I just feel a little ill. Perhaps it was something I ate. I have changed my mind. I do not wish to go to Monsieur Maurepas' house."

The fellow shook his head and grinned.

"No, you must go, Monsieur Croft."

"Why is that?" I asked.

The fellow indicated with his thumb. "Did you not hear him?"

"No," I replied weakly. "What happened?"

"A message from Monsieur Maurepas," he replied. "You are to go to his house this evening. He said it was most urgent."

Too late, I thought, too late now to draw back from the trap opening up before me. Somehow Maurepas must have guessed my secret intentions. I sat biting on my thumb, wondering what to do. I drew out three silver pieces from my purse and gave them to the soldier.

"These are yours, sir. Not a bribe, but a gift."

"For what, Monsieur?"

"You are to take a message before we leave, to either the Abbé Fleury or a man in the palace calling himself Salinet. You are to tell them where I am going and give them this message — 'The hunt is over'."

The fellow took the silver, nodded and slipped out of the door. He made sure it was no trick on my part. I heard the jingle of keys and the lock being turned. I must have waited for a full half-hour. Through the small window in my room I saw the last of the daylight fade and, from the courtyard below, heard the sound of horses' hooves and the creak of carriages as courtiers gathered for another night of revelry. At last, the officer returned, assuring me that my message had been delivered to the Abbé Fleury. I shrugged and stood up, making sure the leather bag was clutched firmly beneath my cloak. I looked round the room for the last time. I would not return there: the small bed, the basin and jug, the chair, all of them silent witnesses to the turmoil I had been through since my arrival in the Louvre Palace. I took the candelabra, blew out the flickering flames and followed the officer downstairs, out of the palace and into the cold night air. All around us there was bustle, the flare of torches, the cultured high-pitched tones of the courtiers and the shrill screams of delight of their ladies. I was torn between anger and fear. Anger at the way I had been trapped, frightened of what was about to happen.

NCE we were clear of the palace grounds and into the narrow, twisting streets I kept looking around, hoping that someone would follow us. Perhaps Fleury had sent Salinet or maybe a detachment of soldiers. I just hoped that some help would arrive. Sometimes I heard the clink of metal or the slither of footsteps behind us, the officer disregarded it, seeming more eager to get his task done than worry about any danger. At last we reached the small cul-de-sac and Maurepas' house. I could see light twinkling between the chinks in the thick velvet curtains and found some joy at the prospect of seeing Marie again. The officer knocked gently on the door and Maurepas opened it. He graciously thanked the officer, ushered me in as if I were some favoured guest and gestured to take my cloak.

"I prefer to keep it on," I snapped.

The archivist smiled.

"You are a strange man, Ralph. Come, Marie is waiting!"

Maurepas took me into the hall which was rather dark and I was surprised that only one candelabra was being used. Marie sat on a tall, throne-like chair before the fire. She rose as I entered, welcoming me with her hands and eyes. Her face looked grave, however, and in the light of the roaring fire I noticed how she had used no paints or perfumes and had a great cloak wrapped about her.

"What is wrong?" I asked. "Are you ill?"

She shook her head rather sadly and gestured for me to sit between her and her father, serving us both with a brimming cup of full claret. We sat drinking the wine, staring into the flames of the roaring fire. I felt strange and deeply uneasy. Why was the room so dark? Why, despite the warmth, did my spine tingle with fear as if some malevolent presence gloated from the darkness?

"You have discovered who the masked man is?" Maurepas asked abruptly.

"Yes, yes," I replied. "I know his true identity and the secrets he carried."

Marie made deft movements with her fingers.

"You are going to tell us?"

I looked at her sad, pretty face. What an actress!

"Why should I tell you?" I replied softly. I touched her hand resting on the arm of the chair; it was ice-cold.

Maurepas straightened in his chair and I stiffened with fear at a sound behind me. My hand went beneath my cloak, caressing the polished handle of the pistol.

"We are your friends, Ralph," Maurepas murmured.

"But I am not working for friends!" I retorted. "We both work for the Regent."

Maurepas turned and looked at me.

How his face had changed. Perhaps it was the shadows which flitted across the room. He looked solemn, ageless, as if he had doffed the disguise of the careful archivist.

"You will tell us, Ralph?"

I grasped the butt of the pistol.

"I will tell you," I said, "when you tell me why you murdered D'Estivet!"

Maurepas just sipped from his wine cup as if we were talking about the death of a pet dog. I looked across at Marie. She was smiling now, running the tip of her tongue around those beautiful kissable lips.

"You did kill him!" I insisted.

Again the deft movements of Marie's fingers.

"How do you know that?"

I gazed into those dark eyes.

"Do you know, Marie," I said, "you were probably the only person D'Estivet liked, perhaps even loved. Yet yours was the last face he saw just before you drove the dagger straight through his heart." I turned to the archivist. "And you, Monsieur Maurepas, you took the body and dumped it where you thought it belonged, on a rubbish heap."

"How do you know, Ralph?" Maurepas answered.

I eased the pistol in my belt.

"Oh," I replied, "it was quite easy. First, you were the last people D'Estivet ever saw. Secondly, D'Estivet was a killer, he roamed the streets of Paris like a panther, his reputation went before him. No one would dare to confront him. Had I been going to murder D'Estivet I would have hired a marksman, the best this city has, and had him kill D'Estivet from far off." I watched Maurepas' face break into a smile. "But, of course," I continued, "D'Estivet was not killed like that, was he? He was killed by someone close to him. Someone he trusted. Anyone else and D'Estivet would have drawn that bloody sword he always carried."

I turned to look at Marie, who smiled coldly back.

"You know," I continued, "D'Estivet

once told me how he slept with his sword and that he only took it off when making love to a woman. I suspect that when he came back late that Friday evening you, Marie, and Maurepas, lured him to his death. I can imagine it now. D'Estivet in his arrogance taking off his sword-belt," my voice rose, "allowing you to caress him. It would only take seconds to take the Italian dagger you had concealed, and plunge it into his heart, turning it once, perhaps twice, and what could D'Estivet do? Scream? Pray? A few seconds of regret before his soul went out into the darkness. Then your father." I turned to where the archivist sat, his chin resting in the palm of his hands, like some Catholic priest listening to a confession. "Your father took the corpse and dumped it. You made one mistake. I realised it tonight when I put my own sword-belt on. You tied D'Estivet's belt the wrong way." I paused. "So why?"

"D'Estivet had to die," Maurepas

murmured. "You see, he was going to betray us, as well as use the secrets we had discovered to blackmail the Regent. Oh, yes," he muttered, as if talking to himself, "he came back that Friday evening full of arrogance and stupidity. He accused us of being members of the Secret Order of the Templars, saying he would use the knowledge about D'Auger to blackmail the Regent and take the money for his own ends. He said Marie also was a part of the bargain. I had to give her to him, otherwise he would accuse us of treason. I stormed out, Marie tried to reason with him." He smiled across at his daughter. "But, as I said, D'Estivet was stupid enough to believe her. He took off his sword-belt, grabbed her, pulling her down on the couch as if she were some city whore!" Maurepas grimaced. "The rest you know!"

"You told me," I said, "that D'Estivet was the Regent's most faithful aide and servant."

"Oh, yes he was," Maurepas replied. "But, like all men, he had his price. He wanted Marie and wanted to give her all the luxuries a lady should have." Maurepas grinned at me. "You know, he was furious when you maintained that D'Auger was not the masked prisoner. You see, D'Estivet thought D'Auger would be scandal enough: the Regent would buy him off and D'Estivet would have Marie because of his allegations that both she and her father were members of a proscribed secret society. I think the Regent suspects me already. Perhaps that is why D'Estivet was told to work with me. At first, we made little progress but then I heard of your imprisonment. After all, Master Croft, as the forger Scaramac, your reputation was well known. You were just the sort of quick-witted rogue we needed." He tweaked me affectionately on the arm. "It was the best decision I have ever made. You were brilliant, Ralph. You have wasted your brains and your talents." He stood up and stretched. "Now, come, tell us what you know."

I took the pistol from beneath my cloak and stared at him while I turned, cocking the hammer, pointing the muzzle directly at Marie.

"I am going to tell you nothing, Monsieur," I replied, nothing at all. Instead, I wish you to bring as much silver and gold as you have. I will fill my purse, slip into the darkness outside and run as fast as I can, whichever way I can, either to a channel port," I smiled, "or perhaps I will go south to Spain. Or maybe Italy. Or the Low Countries. Or the German States."

I glanced at Marie but she just stared back, watching me guardedly.

"And what will you do there?" Maurepas asked.

I turned quickly as he edged closer.

"Do not do anything foolish, Monsieur Maurepas!" I begged. "The pistol is cocked and, though I love your daughter, my finger might slip. It did once before, you know, in a tavern back in Cornwall. Do you realise," I said, "if my finger hadn't slipped I wouldn't be here now."

Maurepas stepped back.

"I asked you, Ralph, what would you do once you fled."

"Oh, I will write out what I know. Give a copy to the nearest French ambassador with the promise that, if a certain sum is paid over to me," I kicked the small leather bag at my feet, "I shall hand back all the documents I have and keep quiet about a secret which would rock the throne of France!"

"The Regent would track you down. There are paid assassins. He or others could hire them."

"That old roué!" I answered. "I doubt if he gives a fig about anything except his own lecherous, incestuous thoughts! And, as for assassins, you forget, Monsieur Maurepas, I can change my name. I can alter my appearance, I can hire men like

299

D'Estivet to protect me, even from the Templars."

The archivist smiled.

"Like he did in the Rue des Bons Enfants?"

I sat down again, resting my elbow on the arm of the chair, the cocked pistol pointing a few inches past Marie's head. (I now confess under no circumstances would I have fired.) "You remember the assassins in the Rue des Bons Enfants?" Maurepas asked again. "They were," he continued, "hired by D'Estivet. You know that?"

I nodded.

"But you don't know the reason why. Shall I tell you? D'Estivet informed the Regent that he believed you had hired the assassins to kill him and make your escape. D'Estivet claimed you were in secret communication with Monsieur Villon and other criminals in the Fauboug Saint-Antoine and that you intended to use the information for purposes of blackmail."

Maurepas sat back in his chair,

stretching his legs before the fire as if he were entertaining an old friend, rather than a man who was threatening to kill his daughter.

"I think the Regent believed D'Estivet," he continued. "That's why you were so closely guarded. And, of course, the pistol you are waving at my daughter is not primed. If you check it, you will find the powder is really no more harmful than coaldust."

I stared at Maurepas, then at his daughter, my mind racing. I had been right about D'Estivet. The three criminals had been hired to build up the picture that I was a blackmailer, whilst D'Estivet portrayed himself as the faithful, courageous servant. Whatever happened, the Regent would not have kept his word and D'Estivet may have been looking forward to enjoying my public execution. The bastard! I was glad he was dead. I looked at Marie and saw her make a very swift movement with her fingers. Perhaps she thought I was not quick enough to decipher it but I did. My wits saved my life. She had given her father an order "If he pulls the trigger, he will die!"

What was the powder I had used? I glanced down at my hand, my palm was sweaty with a streak of dirt. I sighed and threw the pistol to the floor. Maurepas picked it up, pointed at the ceiling, his eyes locked with mine. I held my breath. He pressed the trigger, nothing happened.

"Ralph," he said softly, "please stand and unbuckle your belt."

I looked at him and Marie. I could draw my sword but then, behind me, I heard a tinder strike. I turned, a shadowy figure had emerged. He ignored us all and went round the room lighting the candles hidden there. As the chamber flared into light I gasped in astonishment. Seated along the far wall were a group of figures, all cloaked in white, the cross I had seen D'Estivet make, emblazoned in the centre of their gowns; their hands were gloved in white leather gauntlets and their faces and heads concealed by white masks with slits for the eyes, nose and mouth. They were about twelve in number and had been sitting there throughout my entire conversation, six on either side of a great throne-like chair. The one lighting the candles finished his task and went back to his seat. I looked at the long table where, days earlier, I had banqueted with D'Estivet, Maurepas and his daughter. Now, a huge steel, two-edged sword lay in the middle of the table. At one end was a knight's helmet, the type used years ago in tournaments and jousts, the steel polished until it shone like a mirror. At the other end, just beneath the tip of the sword were a pair of mailed gauntlets, lying over each other in the form of a cross. Now Marie moved, undoing the clasp of her cloak, letting it fall to her feet. She, too, wore a white gown and, staring coolly at me, she stretched behind her head and brought a long, white mask over her face. She went across to the

303

great throne-like chair and sat down in silence whilst her father went and occupied the empty seat beside her. I just stared in astonishment: those figures, sitting there, like a panel of judges, made more terrible by their silence and the pure whiteness of their dress. Maurepas, dressed as he always was, stared back at me.

"Welcome, Ralph Croft!" he intoned. "Welcome to the Supreme Court of the Order of the Templars!" He snapped his fingers, making a gesture with his hands. Two of the white figures rose and came over. Each grasped me by an arm, pulling me over to stand behind the table directly across from where Marie sat. I saw her move her white, gloved hands.

Maurepas translated her words.

"The court is now in session."

"Ralph Croft," Maurepas intoned, "do you have anything to say?"

"Yes." I decided impudence was my best gambit. "Yes, I have a great deal to say, but not to you. The

Abbé Fleury, he knows I am here. He knows I am in danger. Even now, he or his agent, Salinet, will have this house ringed with troops!"

Again Marie made signs with her fingers. Maurepas, watching his daughter carefully, turned back to me.

"I don't think so, Ralph," he murmured. He raised his voice. "Salinet!" The man on my right took off his hood and smiled mischievously at me. Of course, Salinet!

"And the Abbé Fleury?" I asked wearily.

The figure on the left of Maurepas rose, took off his hood and the Abbé Fleury smiled benignly at me.

"You said I should trust you!" I accused him. The priest pursed his lips and walked over to me.

"And I was right, Ralph. Whom could you trust? The Regent? I doubt if he would have kept his word. D'Estivet? He would have killed you!"

"We had to make sure," Maurepas interrupted. "We had to make sure that you did not confide in anyone else. It was a hard task. We also did not want you to run. Do you think you would have got far? Do you think men like the Regent or D'Estivet would have let you, an English forger, make a fool of them?"

The Abbé came forward and dusted a speck of dirt from the hem of his cloak.

"We were watching you all the time, Ralph. As we were D'Estivet. We had great plans for him. We thought he might become one of us but then we found he was actually hunting us, ready to betray not only Monsieur Maurepas but his own lord, the Duke of Orleans. He deserved to die! He tried to violate Marie!"

I looked at the cold, passive figure now enthroned in a white gown.

"I loved you, Marie!" I called out.

She sat impassive as the Abbé Fleury walked back to his own seat.

"I said I loved you, Marie!" I shouted again.

This time she made quick, nimble movements with her fingers.

"Marie says," Maurepas translated, "that she has a kindness and tenderness for you." He smiled. "If she did not, you would be dead."

"What is this?" I said, looking round. "What are you but men and women playing silly games!"

"Silly games!" Maurepas commented. "Oh, no, Ralph, not silly. We are all part of a serious and deadly game. In 1307 Philip Capet ordered the imprisonment, torture and execution of the great Order of the Knights of the Templar. Men, brave knights, who defended the west against Islam, suddenly disappeared into dark dungeons."

Maurepas got up and walked towards me, a fanatic gleam in his eyes.

"It was all done in one night, Ralph. Good, brave soldiers tortured, humiliated and then strung up in market places throughout France like a farmer hangs carrion. Philip bullied the church, the papacy and other monarchs in Europe to follow his example and the great order disappeared. For what?" Maurepas wiped his lips on the back of his hand. "Because the Templars were sodomites? That was a lie! Because they were black magicians? That is blasphemy. No, for two reasons. First, Philip wanted the Templars' wealth and he was refused that. Secondly, and most importantly, he himself applied to be a member of the Templars but was turned away as not being worthy of it."

"That was hundreds of years ago!" I cried. "These are stories, legends."

Maurepas shook his head.

"Oh, no, not legends. Philip had the Grand Master, Jacques de Molay, burnt in the square before Notre Dame cathedral. Just before the pyre was lit, de Molay accused Philip of being a liar, summoning both him and Pope Clement V to answer to him before God's tribunal within a year and a day of his own death." Maurepas cleared his throat. "That prophecy proved correct. We are here to ensure his second prophecy is fulfilled, that Philip's descendants be cursed to the thirteenth generation!" Maurepas turned to look where Marie sat. She made the sign to continue.

"Marie is not my daughter," Maurepas said bluntly. "Her real name is de Molay. She is the descendant of the last Grand Master of the Order of the Templars. She, like her ancestors, has kept alive the curse issued in that Paris square. Look at your history, Ralph," he whispered. "Louis XIV's son died mysteriously, his grandson died mysteriously, Louis XIV's own grandfather, Henry IV, was assassinated. And, before that, virtually every French king died a sudden and mysterious death. Only we, the Templars, know the truth. We arranged their deaths. For we intend to bring the whole royal line crumbling down!"

"And you think the identity of the man in the iron mask will help your cause?"

"Of course," the Abbé Fleury remarked.

"But, Monsieur Abbé," I interrupted. "You are tutor to the young king. You could become a great minister, wield absolute power."

"Perhaps I will," the Abbé smiled. "And, as long as we have the great cause, that will be my aim, as did those others, men like Fouquet. You remember him, Ralph, Louis XIV's Finance Minister? He was a member of our secret order, paid and financed by us and he came to know the great secrets you do but, before he could act, he was imprisoned for life."

"Now you are here," Maurepas interrupted, "you know what Fouquet knew. You have seen the letters of Anne of Austria."

I could have laughed as the final piece of the puzzle was pressed neatly into place.

"You find this amusing, Monsieur Croft?" Maurepas asked tartly. "I assure you . . . "

No, no," I answered hastily. "Now it's all clear. You wanted those letters all the time, didn't you?"

Maurepas nodded.

"If you or anyone else had asked," I commented, "the Regent might have become suspicious, so our good Abbé and his friend, Salinet planted the idea in me. He warned me not to tell Monsieur Maurepas just in case D'Estivet realised there was something suspicious."

No one answered my observation. The Abbé Fleury leaned back in his chair, cracking his fingers softly. I waved my hand along the row of silent, white-robed figures.

"And who are these?" I asked.

"Some you have met," Maurepas answered. "Perhaps passed in a corridor or gallery. They do not concern you. What concerns them is what you know. You are going to tell us, Ralph?"

"And if I do not?"

"There are other ways."

"And if I do tell you?"

Maurepas walked across to the table and put his hand on the hilt of the sword.

"If you do, Ralph, I swear on the cross-hilt of the great sword of the Templars that, after a period of probation, you can become one of us."

I stared at Marie. She made one small sign.

"Ralph, please!"

I agreed. Maurepas ordered a chair to be brought and I sat for a few minutes collecting my thoughts.

"The man in the iron mask," I began, "was a half-brother to Louis XIV. Perhaps even more. He was born of Anne of Austria and his father was no less a person than Mazarin, a cardinal in the Catholic church."

"How do you know that?" Maurepas queried.

"It's quite simple. Louis XIII died in 1643. Mazarin became the Queen's chief minister. They had a son. I suspect Mazarin had the boy smuggled out of the country and sent to England, where he lived under the name of Martin. This was the valet, the confidant of the conspirator, Roux."

I looked up at Maurepas.

"Roux was one of your Order, wasn't he?"

Maurepas nodded.

"Of course. He told a Chapter of our Order, the council of Ten in Venice, that he was on the verge of publishing a great scandal which would rock the throne of France. But you know what happened? He was tried and executed within a few days of his capture. Continue, Ralph!"

"I believe," I replied, "that when Mazarin sent the boy to England he could not resist giving him a name linked to his own. First, there is some similarity between Martin and Mazarin. But the name Martin in France is Martinot and in Italy Martinozzi."

"Of course!" Maurepas interjected. "Martinot and Martinozzi are the names of Mazarin's relatives!"

"Exactly!" I cried. "You may remember that in one of his letters Louis actually referred to the masked prisoner as a valet. In fact, the King was making a joke. First, in England Martinot acted as a valet to the revolutionary Roux. Secondly, Louis XIV was a gambler, a famous card player and, in the parlance of the tables, the title 'Valet' is given to the knave, who of course pretends to be a king."

I stopped to drink from a cup of wine Maurepas handed me.

"I believe that 'Martin' was about twenty-four or twenty-five when he was arrested. He was deported from England by King Charles II. He was 'Eustace D'Auger' at Dieppe and taken into custody to Pignerol under Saint-Mars."

"Why should the English hand him over?" Fleury asked.

"Ah," I replied, "if you read your history, Monsieur Abbé, you will find that in 1669 Louis XIV and Charles II of England signed the secret Treaty of Dover in which Charles promised, in return for a massive annual pension, to bring England under the sphere of Catholic France. I suspect that one of the unwritten clauses of this Treaty was the extradition of the man named Martin. You may remember how Louis XIV told the French ambassador in London that when he announced Roux's capture to King Charles II of England, he was to watch the king's face most closely. I think," I concluded, "that Charles II may have guessed the true identity of this valet Martin whom the French wished so desperately to extradite. You may also remember," I added, "that in the mid-1660s Mazarin sent two of his nieces to Charles II's court. They may have gone as spies, perhaps even to hunt the famous valet down."

"Why the name Eustace D'Auger?"

"Well," I replied, "D'Auger was a red herring. Because of his involvement in the Paris underworld, D'Auger disappeared into the madhouse at Saint Lazare. King Louis and his ministers decided to use his name. Quite a useful ploy," I remarked. "D'Auger had been mixed up in some rather unsavoury business and his name served as an extra veil of security, this explains why Louis gave strict orders to the supervisor of the hospital at Saint Lazare never to allow Eustace D'Auger to write to anyone."

I stopped, drinking greedily from the cup of wine. The entire room fell silent and I could sense the excitement and quiet satisfaction of my listeners. Fleury leaned forward in his chair. "Yes, what you say makes sense," he commented. "We know the masked prisoner was tall and dark. So was Mazarin. He could speak English, a valet from England would, of course, be proficient in the language. He was a valet but also a prince, being the illegitimate son of a queen of France and, of course, he was masked because he bore an uncanny resemblance to Louis himself. But there is more, isn't there Ralph?" he added quickly.

"Oh, yes," I replied. "The masked man was looked after by the same gaoler. I suspect Saint-Mars got to know his true identity. Now, although he and his colleagues called him the Man in the Iron Mask or the ancient Prisoner, or Eustace D'Auger, when they came to write out the death certificate, perhaps as a macabre joke, or because they wished in death to proclaim some of the truth, they gave him the name 'Marciel'." I paused for effect. Each of the masked figures sat like statues. "In the letters of Anne of Austria," I said softly, "the queen refers to people, using different terms. She had two codes for the cardinal. He was either 'La Mer', the Sea; or 'Le Ciel', the Heavens."

Maurepas gave a deep sigh.

"Of course," he muttered. "Put the two phrases together and you have Merciel or Marciel!"

The hooded figures whispered to

each other. Marie raised one gloved, white hand for silence and made signs at Maurepas. The archivist rose and came to stand over me.

"We believe what you tell us, Ralph, is the truth. But how did Louis XIV come to know?"

I shrugged.

"Perhaps he had his agents. Perhaps Mazarin himself, or even his mother confided the secret to him just before they died. However," I continued, "if I were a gambling man, I would wager that a member of your Secret Order, Louis XIV's finance minister, Fouquet, knew the secret. He may have used this to blackmail the cardinal, only that could explain the rapid rise to power of a man from nowhere. Of course, it also explains his downfall. Remember, Fouquet was arrested in the middle of a party and hurried away to life imprisonment. Like the masked prisoner, his passive cooperation was the price he paid for his life."

"And Fouquet, Maurepas muttered,

"was the only person ever allowed to talk to the masked prisoner."

"Of course," I added, "when Louis XIV found that Fouquet's manservant had talked to the masked prisoner, the poor unfortunate was also incarcerated for life."

Maurepas turned to face his companions.

"Brethren," he began as if I no longer existed, "what we have learned makes sense. I believe the Englishman has discovered the true identity of the Man in the Iron Mask. He was the illegitimate son of Anne of Austria and her lover, Cardinal Mazarin. He was extradited from England and the price for his silence was comfortable imprisonment for life. Our so-called Sun King, Louis XIV, could not bring himself to execute his own flesh and blood. You may remember that Louis adored his mother. How could he kill a man who had shared the same womb as himself? Commit the crime of Cain and bring divine vengeance down on himself? At the same time King Louis realised the danger behind the secret. If it could be proved in the courts of Europe that Anne of Austria had one illegitimate child, then it was only a matter of time before people began to ask whether she might have had another, casting doubts on Louis XIV's own legitimacy. This explains the arrest of our long-dead comrade, Nicholas Fouquet, the brutal execution of Roux and Louis' attempts to silence all those who came into contact with his secret half-brother. This included the people who worked in the Bastille, perhaps even his own ministers, men such as Louvois, who died in the most mysterious of circumstances. It also explains," he concluded, "Louis XIV's absorption with his own image, his love of glory, his passion for display. It was his way of grasping more securely the crown of France!"

I think he would have continued but the Abbé Fleury suddenly raised a hand.

"I accept," he called out in a clear voice, "the conclusions Brother Maurepas has drawn but I have watched the Englishman's face. I think there is more! Is there not, Ralph?"

Maurepas turned and looked at me severely.

"Well, Englishman?"

"Quite simple," I replied. "You have touched on it already." I paused to gather my thoughts. I did not care now. This Secret Order was the only sure guarantee of any future safety.

"Tell us," Maurepas repeated, "tell us what you know, Ralph."

"Mazarin was in France," I began, "in the early 1630s. He was befriended by Richelieu. One of the scandal sheets you showed me, Monsieur Maurepas, alleged that when Richelieu introduced the young Mazarin to Anne of Austria, he said 'Surely he reminds you of Buckingham, your Grace?'" I stared at the silent line of white garbed figures. "There are rumours," I continued, "that Buckingham was once the great secret love of Queen Anne. It may well be that Mazarin may not have only been the father of the Man in the Iron Mask but of Louis himself. This is what the masked man may have known."

The assembled group let out almost a collective gasp of astonishment as I warmed to my subject.

"You may remember, Monsieur Maurepas, the stories which stated that Louis XIII was incapable of begetting children. I disagree with you. Perhaps they were right. Moreover, one thing strikes me as strange. In the year 1642/1643 there were more than a remarkable series of coincidences: Louis XIII died, Richelieu died, Anne became Regent and Mazarin was appointed as her chief minister. Some people," I concluded, "may believe such a series of coincidences is unacceptable."

"Are you alleging," Maurepas abruptly asked, "that the deaths of Louis XIII and Richelieu were not due to natural causes?"

I shrugged.

"Perhaps such causes were aided and abetted by a man and a woman who were passionately in love with each other. After their removal from the stage, however, Mazarin and Anne made one dreadful mistake. The Queen became pregnant but the subsequent birth of a male child was carefully hidden and the boy smuggled to England." I leaned back in my chair and stared directly at Marie. "Marie," I concluded, "I know there is nothing else to say. The secret behind the Man in the Iron Mask is, even to me a common Englishman, a dreadful one. But I have one question to ask you. Why is it so important for you and your companions to know this?"

"The answer should be obvious," Maurepas replied. We can use this information to win control over the minds and hearts of those pretenders who wear the crown of France. We work at many levels, Englishman, but have one aim, one thought, to bring

the line of Philip IV crashing down!
Fouquet tried to use it but acted
arrogantly and was caught out. We
shall be more careful. This scandal
will not destroy the crown of France
but we will let the information trickle
out like refuse seeps into clear water.
At the same time we are busy in the
colleges and universities, in the army
and the Faubourg Saint-Antoine and
one day we will shatter the entire
glittering charade you have seen at
the Louvre. A new France will be
born! Perhaps under a more just and
acceptable line of Kings!"

I heard Maurepas out but kept staring
at Marie and continued to do even as
one of the white robed figures began
to douse the candles, turning the room
into total darkness. I expected to die
but Maurepas kept his word. He said
I would be accepted as a novice into
his order and, for a while, I would
spend a long but not uncomfortable
imprisonment here in a chateau miles
from Paris deep in the wooded slopes

of the Loire valley.

My journey began the following day in one of the covered wagons of the Moon People. Maurepas later told me the Regent was furious, issuing warrants and orders for my arrest to every Intendant in France. He will, however, never capture me. Maurepas has sworn that, until the Regent dies and the Abbé Fleury takes over the reins of power, I must stay in my chateau. Maurepas said I should write my memoirs and I have done so, faithfully, as events occurred. (I think they want to ensure also that I have missed nothing out.) I believe they will keep their word. One day soon Maurepas will return to this chateau. Marie might come with him and kiss me softly as she once did before. Perhaps, only then, will they remove this velvet mask from my face.

A FOOT IN THE GRAVE
Bruce Marshall

About to be imprisoned and tortured in Buenos Aires, John Smith escapes, only to become involved in an aeroplane hijacking.

DEAD TROUBLE
Martin Carroll

Trespassing brought Jennifer Denning more than she bargained for. She was totally unprepared for the violence which was to lie in her path.

HOURS TO KILL
Ursula Curtiss

Margaret went to New Mexico to look after her sick sister's rented house and felt a sharp edge of fear when the absent landlady arrived.

THE DEATH OF ABBE DIDIER
Richard Grayson

Inspector Gautier of the Sûreté investigates three crimes which are strangely connected.

NIGHTMARE TIME
Hugh Pentecost

Have the missing major and his wife met with foul play somewhere in the Beaumont Hotel, or is their disappearance a carefully planned step in an act of treason?

BLOOD WILL OUT
Margaret Carr

Why was the manor house so oddly familiar to Elinor Howard? Who would have guessed that a Sunday School outing could lead to murder?